BAD SEEDS

Harper felt a craving for vengeance as he looked at the photographs. Didn't seem right that humanity's outward growth should be paid for by such as these. The salt of the earth thrown away for Earth's sake.

Not for one moment did he doubt that should he come face to face with one of these three he would shoot him down like a rabid dog. It was easier for him than for others to perform such cold-blooded execution; mentally he could *see* the terrible emptiness of the human shell and the thing squirming within.

Three fine young men.

Three rotten apples.

THREE
TO
CONQUER

Eric Frank Russell

A Del Rey Book

BALLANTINE BOOKS • NEW YORK

INTRODUCTION

by Jack L. Chalker*

Whenever anyone asks me who my personal favorite SF writer is, I always respond with Eric Frank Russell (1905–1978), the British author who more than anyone influenced my own writing and direction—as well as that of many other contemporary SF writers. Whenever I feel like escaping into somebody else's world and nothing else seems interesting, I know I can always pick up a Russell novel or story collection and have a really good time.

Three to Conquer addresses a constant Russell theme— the fear that we are property, or can become property, of other alien races or forces. Unlike the Fortean mysterious movers or *Sinister Barrier*'s Vitons, however, this is a straightforward invasion tale in which the problem is not

---

*Jack L. Chalker is a popular science fiction and fantasy author who has been a long-time admirer of the works of Eric Frank Russell and who feels that Russell was a strong influence on his own writing. Most of the facts used in this introduction came from letters written by Russell over the years to Chalker and mutual friends. Chalker's enthusiasm was instrumental in bringing about Del Rey's revival of Russell's work.

whether we are property but how to keep us from becoming property.

What sets *Three to Conquer* apart from the huge library of invasions-from-space stories is the way Russell chose to approach the subject. His Venusian viruses are doubly frightening because they are like the alien in John W. Campbell's *Who Goes There*, except in a modern society rather than a remote Arctic base. They infest our bodies and own them, yet they have access to all our memories and are perfect mimics. Russell realized, as Campbell had, that these invaders would be unstoppable in a modern city because they could not be detected until it was too late. But since Russell wanted a story of this horror loose in civilization he required someone who could recognize them instantly for what they were. So, partly thanks to his primary editor John Campbell's then current interest in ESP, he chose a telepath; and for his exposition he selected almost a Chandleresque style.

Three to Conquer stands most on its central character and narrator. He has an extraordinary power, yes, but it is more curse than blessing and he hides it from everyone. He is, in fact, as much of an outsider as the aliens, and with as much to fear from the government. The novel works because *he* works as a real human being. By making this not just a cracking good thriller but also the story of a fascinating and somewhat tragic individual, he sets the book apart from others of its school. Telepathy may be no more real than alien viruses, but it is real here, and how believable it is shows the true genius of Eric Frank Russell.

*'Tis all a Chequer-board of Nights and Days
Where Destiny with Men for Pieces plays:
Hither and thither moves...*

Chapter 1

He was a squat man with immense breadth of shoulder, hairy hands, bushy eyebrows. He maintained constant, unblinking attention on the road as he drove into trouble at sixty miles an hour.

It was April 1, 1980. All Fools' Day, he thought wryly. They had two or three moving roadways in Los Angeles, Chicago and New York. Also six airtight stations up there on the Moon. But except for rear engines and doped-alcohol fuel, motor-cars were little different from those of thirty years ago. Helicopters remained beyond reach of the average pocket. Taxpayers still skinned themselves month after month—and brooded over it every All Fools' Day.

For the past ten years there had been talk of mass produced helicopters at two thousand dollars apiece. Nothing had ever come of it. Maybe it was just as well considering the likely death-roll when drunks, half-wits and hot-rod enthusiasts took to the skies.

For the same ten years the scientific write-up boys had

been forecasting a landing upon Mars within the next five. Nothing had come of that either. Sometimes he doubted whether anything ever would come of it. A minimum of sixty million miles is a terrible distance for a gadget that squirts itself along.

His train of thought snapped when an unknown voice sounded within his peculiar mind saying, *"It hurts! Oh, God, it . . . hurts!"*

The road was wide and straight and thickly wooded on both sides. The only other vehicle in sight was a lumbering tanker mounting a slight slope two miles ahead. A glance in the rear-view mirror confirmed that there was nothing behind. Despite this, the squat man registered no surprise.

"Hurts!" repeated the voice, weakening rapidly. *"Didn't give me a chance. The bastards!"*

The squat man slowed until his speedometer needle trembled under twenty. He made a dexterous U-turn, drove back to a rutted dirt road leading into the woods. He nosed the car up the road, knowing full well that the voice had come from that direction.

In the first five hundred yards there were two sharp bends, one to the right, one to the left. Around the second bend a car stood squarely in the middle of the road, effectively blocking it to all comers. The squat man braked hard, slewed his bonnet over the grass verge to avoid a collision.

He got out, leaving his door open. Speculatively he eyed the other car while he stood still and listened with his mind rather than with his ears.

"Betty . . ." whispered the eerie voice. *"Three fellows and a pain in the guts. Darkness. Can't get up. Ought to tell Forst. Where are you, Forst?"*

Turning, the squat man ran heavily along the verge, clambered down a short bank, found the man in the ditch. He did not look long, not more than two seconds. Mounting the bank with furious haste, he dug a flask out of his car-pocket, took it down to him.

Raising the other's head he poured a thin trickle of spirit between pale lips. He did not say anything, asked no questions, uttered no words of comfort and encouragement. Cradling the head on his forearm he tried only to maintain the fading spark of life. And while he did it, he listened. Not with his ears.

"Tall, blond guy," murmured the other's mind, coming from a vast distance. *"Blasted at me ... others got out ... slung me off the road. Betty, I'm ..."*

The mental stream cut off. The squat man dropped his flask, lowered the other's head, examined him without touching. Dead beyond doubt. He made note of the number on the badge fixed to the uniform jacket.

Leaving the body in the ditch he went to the stalled car, sat in the driver's seat, found a hand-microphone, held it while he fiddled tentatively with switches. He was far from sure how the thing operated but intended to find out.

"Hello!" he called, working a likely lever. "Hello!"

Immediately a voice responded, "State police barracks, Sergeant Forst."

"My name is Wade Harper. Can you hear me?"

"Barracks," repeated the voice, a trifle impatiently. "Forst speaking."

Evidently he couldn't hear. Harper tried again, got something adjusted. "Hello! Can you hear me?"

"Yes. What goes on there?"

"I'm calling from Car Seventeen. One of your officers is dead in a ditch near by." He gave the badge number.

There sounded a quick intake of breath, then, "That's Bob Alderson. Where are you now?"

Harper gave it in detail, added, "He's been shot twice, once in the belly and once through the neck. It must have happened recently because he was still living when I got to him. He died in my arms."

"Did he tell anything?"

"Yes; a tall, fair-haired fellow did it. There were others with him, no number stated, no descriptions."

"Were they in a car?"

"He didn't say, but you can bet on that."

"Stay where you are, Mr. Harper. We'll be right out."

There sounded a sharp click and a new voice broke in with, "Car Nine, Lee and Bates. We picked that up, Sarge, and are on our way. We're two miles off."

Replacing the microphone, Harper returned to the top of the bank, gazed moodily down upon the body. Somebody named Betty was going to know heartbreak this night.

Within a few minutes heavy tyres squealed on the main artery, a car came into the dirt road. Harper raced round the bend, signalled it down lest it hit the block. Two state troopers piled out. They had the bitter air of men who owed somebody plenty and intended to pay it with interest.

They went down into the ditch, came up, said, "He's gone all right. Some son of a bitch is going to be sorry."

"I hope so," said Harper.

The taller of the two surveyed him curiously and asked, "How did you happen to find him way up here?"

Harper was prepared for that. He had practised the art of concealment since childhood. At the ripe age of nine he had learned that knowledge can be resented, that the means of acquiring it can be feared.

"I wanted to pay dog-respects to a tree. Found this car planted in the road. First thing I thought was that somebody else had the same idea. Then I heard him moan in the ditch."

"Five hundred yards is a heck of a long way to come just for that," observed the tall one, sharp-eyed and shrewd. "Fifty would have been enough, wouldn't it?"

"Maybe."

"How much farther would you have gone if the road hadn't been blocked?"

"Couldn't say." He shrugged indifferently. "A fellow just

4

looks for a spot that strikes his fancy and stops there, doesn't he?"

"I wouldn't know," said the trooper.

"You ought to," said Harper. "Unless you are physically unique."

"What d'you mean by that?" asked the trooper, showing sudden toughness.

The second trooper chipped in with, "Lay off, Bert. Ledsom will be here any minute. Let him handle this. It's what he's paid for."

Bert grunted, went silent. The pair started hunting around for evidence. In short time they found fresh tyre-tracks across a soft patch twenty yards higher up the road. Soon afterwards they discovered a shell in the grass. They were examining the shell when three more cars arrived.

A man with a bag got down into the ditch, came up after a while, said wearily, "Two bullets about .32 calibre. Either could have caused death. No burn marks. Fired from range of a few yards. The slugs aren't in him."

Another with captain's chevrons spoke to the two nearest troopers. "Here's the ambulance—lift him out of there." To several others, "You boys look for those slugs. We've *got* to find them." To Lee and Bates he said, "Put a plank over those tracks. We'll make moulage casts of them. See if you can pick up the other shell. Work up the road for the gun as well: the punk may have thrown it away."

He joined Harper, informed, "I'm Captain Ledsom. It was smart of you to use Alderson's radio to get us."

"Seemed the sensible thing to do."

"People don't always do the sensible thing, especially if they're anxious not to be involved." Ledsom surveyed him with cool authority. "How did you find Alderson?"

"I trundled up here to answer the call of nature. And there he was."

"Came up quite a piece, didn't you?"

"You know how it is. On a narrow track like this you tend to look for a spot where you can turn the car to go back."

"Yes, I guess so. You wouldn't want to park on a bend either." He appeared satisfied with the explanation but Harper could see with complete clarity that his mind suspected everyone within fifty miles radius. "Exactly what did Alderson say before he passed out?"

"He mumbled about Betty and—"

"His wife," interjected Ledsom, frowning. "I hate having to tell her about this."

"He mentioned a big, blond fellow blasting at him. Also that there were others who tossed him into the ditch. He gave no more details unfortunately. He was on his last lap and his mind was rambling."

"Too bad." Ledsom shifted attention as a trooper came up. "Well?"

"Cap, the tracks show that a car turned up here with Alderson following. The car stopped by the verge. Alderson pulled up behind but in the middle of the road. He got out, went toward the first car, was shot down. At least two men picked him up and dumped him out of sight." He held out his hand. "Here's the other shell." He pointed. "It was lying right there."

".32 automatic," said Ledsom, studying the small brass cylinders. "Any sign of Alderson's car having been edged off the road and put back again?"

"No."

"Then they must have pushed straight ahead. They couldn't get out this way with that car stuck across the road." He rubbed his chin thoughtfully and went on, "This track meanders seventeen miles through forest, loops back and joins the main artery about ten miles farther along. So by now they've either got back on the road or they've holed up someplace in the woods."

"Seventeen miles would take at least twenty minutes on

a route like this one," ventured Harper. "Even if they're driving like crazy they can't be far off it yet."

"Yes, I know. I'll call the boys to put up roadblocks along the main run. We'll search the loop too. It's used almost entirely by loggers. If those bums are familiar with it the chances are they work or once worked for the logging outfits. We'll follow that line later."

Entering his car, Ledsom spoke awhile on the radio. He came back, said, "That's fixed. Blocks will be established pretty soon. Local sheriff is on his way here with four deputies." He gazed moodily at the surrounding woods. "Just as well they're coming. The fugitives may dump that car and take to their feet, in which case we'll need an army to go through this lot."

"Any way I can help?" asked Harper.

Ledsom looked him over for the third time, carefully, calculatingly, while his mind said to itself, *"Some crazy coot might think it incontrovertible proof of innocence to stick his head in the lion's mouth. I'd like to know more about this guy. All we've got to go on so far is* his *story."*

"Well?" encouraged Harper.

"Finding the murder weapon could give us a lead," remarked Ledsom in the manner of one idly musing. "And we can't afford to overlook any possibility, no matter how remote." Then his eyes stared straight into Harper's and his voice became sharp, imperative. "Therefore we must search you and your car."

"Naturally," responded Harper with bland indifference.

"Wrong diagnosis," decided Ledsom's mind. *"He's clean. We'll frisk him all the same."*

They raked the car from end to end, ran hands over Harper, extracted a tiny blued automatic from his right-hand pocket. Ledsom grabbed the gun eagerly, ejected the magazine from the hand-grip, examined it, jerked his eyebrows a bit.

"Holy smoke! What sort of a rod is this supposed to be?

Twenty in the mag with slugs the size of match-heads. Where did you get it?"

"Made it myself. Up to fifty yards it is very effective."

"I can imagine. You got a permit for it?"

"Yes." Harper produced it, handed it over.

Ledsom glanced at it, registered more surprise. "Are you a Federal agent?"

"No, Captain. The F.B.I. issued that for reasons of their own. If you want the reasons you'll have to ask them."

"No business of mine," said Ledsom, a little baffled. He handed back the permit and the gun. "That toy isn't the weapon we want, anyway. Did you see or hear anything suspicious before or after finding Alderson?"

"Not a thing."

"No sound of a car beating it, for instance?"

"No sound whatever."

"You didn't hear the shots before you arrived?"

"No."

"Umph!" Ledsom was dissatisfied. "So they had at least two or three minutes headstart. You're a material witness and we want a statement from you at the office. Sorry to put you to more trouble and delay but—"

"Only too glad to assist," said Harper.

Ledsom directed two crews to explore the loop road then led the way back to barracks. Reaching his office, he slumped behind his desk; sighed deeply.

"It's a lousy business. I've yet to tell his wife. They hadn't been married that long, either. God knows how she'll take it." He sighed again, dug an official form out of a drawer. "Have to do some clerking myself, seeing all the boys are busy. You got a card on you, Mr. Harper?"

Harper slid one across to him.

It read: WADE HARPER—FORGER.

"So help me Mike," said Ledsom, blinking at it. "That's what I call advertising one's sins. Next thing one of them will write me on a business sheet headed *Baldy O'Brien—Heistman*."

"I'm a microforger."

"What sort of animal is that?"

"I make surgical and manipulatory instruments so tiny they can be used to operate on a bacillus."

"Oh, now, don't give me that!" said Ledsom. "A fellow couldn't see enough to use them."

"He can—under a powerful microscope."

"Every year they think up something new," marvelled Ledsom. "You can't keep up with it."

"There's nothing new about this," Harper assured. "It started back in 1899 with a Dutchman named Dr. Schouten. Since then the only considerable improvement on his technique has been gained by de Fonbrune's one-hand pneumatic micromanipulator. I make variations on that gadget, too."

"You must be kept mad busy," remarked Ledsom, wondering how many or how few people wanted to dissect a germ.

"I get by. There aren't more than a couple of dozen competent microforgers in the world. The demand is just enough to keep pace with the supply."

"So the F.B.I. thinks they can't afford to lose you?"

"You're making guesses," said Harper.

"This bacteriological warfare business, maybe?"

"You're still guessing."

"Okay. I know when to mind my own business."

He got to work on the official form, put down the witness's name, address and occupation, followed it with a dictated account of what had occurred, shoved it across for the other to read and sign.

When Harper had gone, Ledsom grabbed the phone, made a long distance call. He'd just finished talking when Sergeant Forst entered the office, eyed him curiously.

"Something broken, Cap?"

"That Harper guy fed me a line that would do credit to

the best con man in the biz. So I just called his hometown to see if he has a record."

"And he has?"

"Yes."

"Jumping Judas!" said Forst, dropping a couple of books on the desk and making for the door. "I'll put out a pick-up call for him."

"No." Ledsom looked pensive. "His hometown cops send him love and kisses. He's helped them solve several tough cases and he's shot down three culprits for good measure."

"What is he, a private dick?"

"Nothing like that. They say he has a habit of falling headlong over something everybody else is looking for. They say he's done it time and again and it's uncanny." He sought for a satisfactory theory, found it, ended, "Reckon he suffers from beginner's luck and makes a hobby of exploiting it."

If the subject of conversation had been within half a mile he'd have picked up that notion and smiled.

Driving at fast pace along the main road Harper passed through three successive road-blocks without incident. His mind was working as he tooled along. If, he argued, a chased car switched into a sidetrack the odds would be at least fifty to one on the driver choosing a turn-off on his own side rather than one across the artery and on the far side. The choice would be automatic or instinctive.

Since he was now running with the loop-road somewhere ahead and on his wrong side it was very likely that Alderson and the chased car had come from the opposite direction, or towards him.

He glanced at his watch. It said six-twenty. He had found Alderson at four-ten, a little over two hours ago. That could put the murderers best part of a hundred miles away if they'd kept going nonstop. Probably the police had road-blocks farther out than that. Probably police had been alerted over a huge area by an eight-state alarm.

It wouldn't do much good. There was no adequate description of the fugitives, none at all of their car. A tall, blond fellow just wasn't enough to go upon. About the only chance the police had of making a quick pinch lay in the possibility that the escapees were using a stolen vehicle that some sharp-witted officer might recognize as a wanted number.

He let a few miles go by until he saw a service-station on the opposite side, the side that in his theory Alderson and the killers had used. He crossed, pulled up near the pumps. Two attendants came over.

"Were you fellows on duty around four o'clock?"

Both nodded.

"See anything of a prowl car driven by a trooper named Alderson? Car Seventeen, it was."

"I know Bob Alderson," said one. "He was around a couple of times this morning."

"Not between three and four?"

"No." He thought a bit. "Or if he was I didn't see him."

"Me neither," said the other.

Their minds told that they spoke truth. Harper knew it with absolute sureness. So far as he was concerned they need not have opened their mouths.

"Anyone else here who might have noticed him around that time?"

"Only Satterthwaite. Want me to ask him?"

"I'd appreciate it."

The attendant went out of sight around the back of the building. It made no difference. Harper could hear them mentally though their voices were out of reach.

"Hey, Satty, a fellow here wants to know if you saw anything of Bob Alderson two or three hours back."

"Nary a sign."

He came back. "No luck, Satty didn't see him."

"Anyone now off-duty who was here at that time?"

"No, mister." He showed curiosity. "Like me to tell Bob you're looking for him if he happens to come along?"

"He won't be along—ever," said Harper.

"What d'you mean?"

"Some hoodlum shot him down around four. He's dead."

"Gee!" said the attendant, going pale.

"You'll have the police here asking similar questions sooner or later." Harper gazed up the road. "Know of any place on his patrol where Alderson was in the habit of stopping awhile?"

"He'd often grab a coffee at the Star Café."

"Where's that?"

"Four miles along, on the cross-roads."

"Thanks."

He pulled out, drove fast. Two miles farther on and halfway to the café stood another filling station, this time on his own side of the road. Turning into there, he put the same questions.

"Sure I saw him," said a laconic, sandy-haired youth. "Didn't notice the time but it must have been about three hours back."

"Was he chasing somebody?"

The other considered this, said, "Yes, now that I come to think of it maybe he was."

"What happened?"

"One of those low-slung green Thunderbugs went past in a hell of a hurry and he came half a mile behind like he'd no time to waste either."

"But you aren't positive that he was pursuing the Thunderbug?"

"I didn't think so at the time. Most of the stuff on this road moves good and fast, but now that you mention it I guess he may have been after that car."

"Did you notice who was in it?"

"Can't say that I did."

"Did anyone else see this too? Was anyone with you at the time?"

"No."

Harper thanked him and pushed on. So far he'd gained one item: a green Thunderbug. He didn't congratulate himself on that. He'd shown no especial cleverness in picking up this datum. Of a surety the police would find it themselves before the night was through. He was one jump ahead of them solely because he was concentrating on one specific line of search while they were coping with a hundred. Harper had great respect for the police.

At the Star Café a pert waitress reported that Alderson had eaten a meal there and left about one-thirty. Yes, he'd been by himself. No, he hadn't shown particular interest in any other customers or departed coincidentally with anyone else. No, she hadn't seen a tall, blond fellow with a green Thunderbug.

She hadn't noticed which direction Car Seventeen had taken but she'd ask the other girls. She went away, came back, said that one named Dorothy had seen Alderson go up the left-hand cross-road.

Harper took that road, kept the accelerator pedal well down. Fifteen minutes later he found a tavern keeper who had seen Car Seventeen rocketing along at sometime after three. This witness said he had been drawn to the window by the noise of a car going hell for leather. The car had shot past before he could get a view of it but he'd been in time to see Alderson racing by. Yes, he had thought at the time that Alderson was after someone, probably a daft kid in a hot-rod.

Seven miles farther on Harper struck oil. It was at another filling station. An elderly man came out, handed him news worth having.

"Shortly after three a Thunderbug hauled up to the pumps for ten gallons of alk. There were three fellows and a girl in it. The girl was sitting in the back with one of the fellows and she kept giving me funny sort of appealing looks through the window while I stood near by with the hose in the gas-tank. I had an idea that she wanted to scream but didn't dare. The whole set-up looked decidedly fishy to me."

"What did you do about it?"

"Nothing at that moment. I was by myself and I'm not as young as I used to be. Those three could have bounced me on my nut until my brains fell out."

"So what then?"

"They paid and pushed off without realizing that they'd given me the fidgets. I'd been acting natural because I didn't want any trouble. But as soon as they'd got up a bit of speed I skipped into the road for a look at their plates."

"Did you get the number?" asked Harper, hoping to be dealt an ace out of the pack.

"No. I'd left it a mite too late. I hadn't my glasses on and the figures were too fuzzy to read." The oldster frowned, regretting the lost opportunity. "Couple of minutes later a prowl car came along at easy pace. I flagged it down, told the trooper about this girl. He said he'd look into the matter. He went after the Thunderbug at a good clip." His rheumy eyes quested hopefully. "Did he latch on to something?"

"Yes—a coffin. They plugged him in the neck and belly. He didn't take long to die."

"Good God!" The oldster was visibly shaken. He swallowed hard, said with morbid self-reproach, "And I sent him after them."

"It isn't your fault, Pop. You did the best thing in the circumstances." Harper waited a minute for the other to recover, then asked, "Did those fellows say anything to indicate where they'd come from or where they were going?"

"They spoke exactly one word and no more. The big blond only dropped his window and said, 'Ten!' I asked about oil and water but he shook his head impatiently. Nobody else made any remark. The girl looked as if she'd talk plenty once she got started but was too scared to begin."

"What did this bunch look like? Give me as complete and detailed a description as you can manage."

The other licked his lips and said, "The blond one was doing the driving. He was a husky guy in his late twenties, yellow hair, blue eyes, strong chin, clean-shaven, good-looking and intelligent. You'd have called him a nice kind of fellow if his eyes hadn't been meaner than a snake's."

"No facial scars or other identifying marks?"

"Not that I noticed. Tell you what, though—he was pale. So were the other two guys. You know, whitish, like they get when they've been bottled up quite a piece." He gave Harper a significant glance. "Seeing what's happened I can think up a reason for that."

"So can I. They've just come out of clink. They've escaped or been paroled, more likely the former judging by the way they're acting."

"That's how it looks to me."

"Had they been hitting the booze?" inquired Harper, sensing a possible lead at wherever the stuff had been bought.

"Far as I could tell they were cold sober."

"What else can you add?"

"The fellow sitting alongside the driver was another husky about the same age. Black hair, grey eyes, clean-shaven. He was just as pale-faced, just as mean-looking. I never got a proper look at the third one in the back."

"How about the girl?"

"Around twenty or twenty-one, brown eyes, brown hair, a bit on the plump side. Attractive without being a stunner. Wearing a mustard-coloured overcoat, yellow blouse and a string of amber beads. Her hand was up by the window and she had a birthday ring with an opal in it."

"Somebody born in October. You're doing top-notch, Pop."

"Like I told you, I noticed that girl," said the oldster.

15

"How were the fellows dressed?"

"All the same; dark green jackets, grey shirts and collars, dark green ties. Looking almost as if they wore uniform with buttons and insignia removed. Never seen anyone wearing that sort of rig-out. Have you?"

"No," admitted Harper. "It doesn't resemble prison garb either. Maybe it's sporting togs they've swiped from some store." He continued his cross-examination a few more minutes, finished with, "Have you a telephone here?"

"Sure. Come round the back." He led the way, pointed. "There you are—help yourself."

The voice in the earpiece growled, "State police barracks. Captain Ledsom."

"My lucky day," remarked Harper, unconsciously confirming theories at the other end. "You're the very man I want."

"Who's speaking?"

"Harper. Remember me?"

"Ah, so you've thought up something you forgot to tell us?"

"I gave you all I had at that sorry time. I've since dug up a bit more."

"Such as what?"

"The car you want is a recent model green Thunderbug carrying three fellows and a girl. I have descriptions of all but one of the men."

Ledsom exploded, "Where the blazes did you get all this?"

Grinning to himself, Harper told him where and how.

"Why don't you join the cops and have done with it, instead of fooling around with germ-chivvying gadgets?" Ledsom demanded.

"Because I'm a couple of inches too short, six inches too wide, detest discipline and want to go on living."

Giving a deep grunt, Ledsom said, "I'll send a car out there right away. Maybe the boys will pick up something else. Meanwhile you'd better give me the dirt you've collected."

Harper recited it, finished, "Obviously there are now two leads I couldn't follow even if I wanted. They are properly your work because you have the facilities. Firstly, have any three fellows answering these descriptions been let out of prison or climbed the walls recently? Secondly, has any young girl answering this description been reported missing of late?"

A tolerant chuckle sounded before Ledsom replied, "We'll tend to those and about six more angles you've missed."

"For example."

"Where did they get the clothes they're wearing, the money they're spending, the car they're using, the gun they fired?" He was quiet a moment, then continued, "We'll send out a flier that may bring us the answers from some place. With luck we'll learn the tag-numbers on that Thunderbug. Ten to one it's stolen."

"I could push on along this route and perhaps learn more," said Harper. "They may have stopped for beer or a meal and talked out of turn within somebody's hearing. But why should I bother? What do I pay taxes for? I have business of my own to do."

"You're arguing with yourself, not with me," Ledsom pointed out. "Nobody's asking or expecting you to do anything." He hurried on with, "Of course we really do appreciate the part you've played so far. It shows fine public spirit. Things would be easier for us if everyone were as helpful."

Harper removed the phone from his ear, stared at it suspiciously, put it back, said, "Why can't they have visiscreens on these things in rural areas too?"

"What has that to do with anything?"

"One could watch a guy's expression while he's plastering on the butter." He hooked the phone, turned, said to the oldster, "They're coming straight out. You'd better spend the interim stewing the matter and see if you can recall any item you may have overlooked. They'll need everything you can give them."

Returning to his car, he set about his normal affairs confident that so far as he was concerned the episode was finished. He was out of it, no more involved in it, a momentary witness who had paused and passed on.

He could not have been more wrong.

Chapter 2

He stopped at the next town, found a suitable hotel, booked a room for the night, took in a third-rate show during the evening. He listened to the midnight news before going to bed but it made only brief mention of the killing plus the usual soothing statement that the police hoped to make an early arrest.

The stereoscopic video—called by all and sundry "the pane" since the day a famous cynic had defined the self-styled "window on the world" as "a pane in the neck"— gave the murder a little more attention with pics of troopers and deputies searching the loop-road.

Both radio and video were more interested in vagaries of the weather, sports results, the round-the-globe rocket race, and a complicated legal battle between the government and the Lunar Development Company. According to the latter the government was trying to use its Earth-Moon transport monopoly to bludgeon the L.D.C. into handing itself over complete with fat profits. The L.D.C. was fighting back. It was the decades-old struggle of private enterprise against bureaucratic interference.

Harper sat out this last part in the role of a spectator foreseeing his own fate should he grow too big and become too prosperous. In his line of business he'd had a lot to do with officialdom, but fortunately the basis had been co-operative rather than dictatorial. Nevertheless he sympathized with L.D.C.

He had a sound sleep, arose at eight, breakfasted, spent the morning at the Schultz-Masters Research Laboratories where they needed certain special micromanipulators and displayed the flattering attitude that only he could make them. At one o'clock he left with two tough technical problems solved, two more yet to be considered, and a provisional order in his pocket.

After a meal he started homeward and at three-thirty was halted by a prowl car at a point forty miles from the scene of yesterday's shooting. One of the two troopers in the car got out and came towards him.

He watched the approach with surprised interest and because the oncomer's mind was warily broadcasting *"Maybe and maybe not, but if so he won't get away with it* THIS *time!"*

"Something wrong?" Harper asked.

"You Wade Harper?"

"Yes."

"A call went out for you half an hour ago. Captain Ledsom wants to see you."

"I saw him yesterday."

"This is today," the trooper reminded.

"Can I talk to him on your short-wave?"

"He wants you in person."

"Any idea why?"

The other shrugged. His mind showed that he did not know the reason but viewed Harper as a major suspect merely because he was wanted. It showed also that he and his companion were ready to cope in effective manner with any refusal.

"Mean to say I've got to take time off and go all the way to the barracks?"

"That's how it is." He made an authoritative gesture with an added touch of impatience. "Turn her around and get going. Make it a steady pace, not too fast, and no monkey tricks. We'll be right behind."

Feeling rather peeved, Harper did as instructed. It wasn't that he was in a great hurry, in fact he had time to spare, but he disliked being given peremptory orders by a wide-open mind devoid of adequate motive.

He had been the same in this respect since he'd worn rompers. Perceptive mind resented dictatorship by non-perceptive mind. To do exactly as he was told smacked of the sighted being led around by the blind.

Occasionally, in introspective moments, he chided himself for his mutinous tendencies lest the fact that he'd been mentally alone, completely without intimate contact with a mind similar to his own, should be giving him a superiority complex born of a sense of uniqueness. He had no desire to be humble, he had less desire to be sat upon. He was a seeker of the middle way.

Tramping unwillingly into Ledsom's office, he thumped himself into a seat that creaked, stared belligerently across the desk and read the other's change of viewpoint as easily as an ordinary person reads a book.

"Well, here I am."

Ledsom said pointedly, "We're having a tape-recording this time." Leaning sidewise, he switched on the apparatus. "Where were you the night before last?"

"At an hotel."

"Which one?"

Harper told him.

"What time did you leave there?" Ledsom inquired.

"At nine-thirty."

"Where did you spend the morning?"

"At the Pest Control Station."

"Until when?"

"Close on one o'clock. I then had dinner."

"Where?"

"At the Cathay, a Chinese restaurant."

"With whom?"

"Nobody. I was by myself. Say, what's behind all this?" The question was pure concealment. He already knew what was behind it because he could watch Ledsom's brains fizzing.

"Never mind, Mr. Harper. Just you answer the questions. You have nothing to fear, have you?"

"Who hasn't? Any minute Gabriel may blow his horn."

"You know what I mean." Ledsom eyed him without the friendliness of yesterday. "At what time did you leave the Cathay?"

"About two o'clock, give or take five minutes."

"And after that?"

"I headed for Hainesboro. I had business to do there today at the Schultz-Masters place."

"You came this way?"

"Of course. It's on the direct route."

"You were passing the loop-road about when?"

"Four o'clock."

"Now tell me exactly what happened from that point onward."

"Oh, Lord! I gave you the whole story yesterday. You've got it in writing."

"I know. And now we want it again." Ledsom's mind added with mistaken secretiveness, *"A liar needs a good memory. This is where we find contradictions in his story, if any."*

Harper went grimly through the account for the second time while the tape-recorder purred on. It was the same in all details. He knew it and also that Ledsom knew it.

"About that trick gun you've got," said Ledsom. "You wouldn't be in the habit of carrying a second one such as a .32, would you?"

"No, I wouldn't."

"There's a large pond of considerable depth in the woods about fifty yards from where Alderson was killed. Did you notice it?"

"I didn't enter the woods."

"Did you know of the pond's existence?"

"No."

"You told us you went up that road for a certain purpose. Presumably you were balked by what you discovered. Did you achieve that purpose?"

"I did."

"When?"

"After I'd called Forst on the radio."

"You found Alderson, called the police and then went into the woods?"

"It wasn't necessary to go into the woods, there being no ladies present."

Ignoring that point, Ledsom went on, "At what time did you leave your hotel yesterday morning?"

"You've asked that one before. Nine-thirty."

"And you were all morning where?"

"At the Pest Control Station. If you're trying to catch me out you're wasting time and breath. We can go on this way for a week."

"All right," said Ledsom, changing tactics. "If you had a deal in prospect with Schultz-Masters why didn't you go there until today?"

Harper gave a resigned sigh and said, "Firstly, because my appointment was for today and not for yesterday. Secondly, I reached Hainesboro too late for any business calls, in fact it was already too late when I left here."

"That's what interests us," informed Ledsom, gazing at him steadily. "You'd been badly delayed by the time we finished with you. All the same, you took time off to hunt up four people in a Thunderbug. Why did you do that?"

"Alderson died in my arms. I didn't like it."

Ledsom winced but kept firmly to the issue. "Is that your only reason?"

"It's the major one."

"What's a minor one?"

"My day was messed up. A couple of hours one way or the other couldn't make any difference."

"No other motives whatsoever?"

"One," admitted Harper reluctantly.

"Name it."

"I got some personal satisfaction out of finding a trace on the killers myself."

"*If* they *were* the killers," commented Ledsom. He switched off the recorder, meditated a minute, continued, "Up to a couple of hours ago I didn't doubt it. Now I'm not so sure." He kept his full attention on his listener, watching for reactions. "We're pumping out that pond. Maybe we'll find the gun and learn who used it."

"Meaning me?"

"I haven't said so."

"You're hinting at it with every muscle in your face." Harper made a gesture of disparagement. "I can't blame you in the least for suspecting anyone and everyone. I could have killed Alderson. The time, the place and the opportunity all fit in. Only things lacking are the gun and the motive. You're going to have a hell of a time tying a motive on to me. I had never seen Alderson in my life until that moment."

"We had a senseless killing near here four years ago," answered Ledsom. "Two brothers fell out over an incredibly trivial matter, got equally stubborn about it, gradually switched from argument to abuse and from there to mutual challenges. Finally the hotter tempered of the two upped and slugged the other, killed him, made a very clever try

24

at concealing his guilt by distracting attention elsewhere. He almost succeeded—but not quite!"

"So I followed Alderson into a lane, stopped behind him, swapped backchat. One word led to another. Being cracked, I shot him twice, threw the gun into a pond, called you to come take a look." Harper pulled a wry face. "Time I had my head examined."

"I can't afford to overlook any possibilities," Ledsom gave back. "I've just asked you a lot of questions. Are you willing to take them again with a lie-detector?"

"Positively not!"

Ledsom breathed deeply and said, "You realize that we must attach a certain significance to your refusal?"

"You can tie a couple of tin cans on to it for all I care. The polygraph is an outrageous piece of pseudo-scientific bunkum and its needle-wagglings aren't admissable as legal evidence."

"It has helped extract a few confessions," declared Ledsom, on the defensive.

"Yes, from the babes and sucklings. I am a maker of top-grade scientific instruments myself. You drag a polygraph into court and I'll tear it to pieces for all time."

That worried Ledsom. His thoughts revealed that he believed Harper perfectly capable of it and peculiarly competent to do it. He dismissed the lie-detector as a blunder and wished he had never mentioned it.

"How about scopomaline?" suggested Harper, for good measure. "I'll talk that right out of usage if you'll give me half a chance." He leaned forward, knowing that their respective positions were reversed even if only momentarily, that for a few seconds he was the inquisitor and Ledsom the culprit. "From the criminal viewpoint what have I got that those punks in the Thunderbug haven't got? Do you regard them as figments of my imagination and think I've bribed witnesses to support my story?"

"They were real enough. We have proof of that."

25

"Well, then?"

"Two hours ago we picked up the girl. Her story doesn't jibe with yours. Somebody's a liar."

Lying back in his seat, Harper eyed him meditatively, said, "So you've got the girl. Is her version a trade secret?"

Ledsom thought it over, decided that there was nothing to lose. "She missed her bus, thumbed a lift. Three fellows picked her up in that green Thunderbug. They were in a humorous mood, took her a long, roundabout way, kidded her she was being kidnapped. At that filling station she really was scared, but after a bit more fooling around they dumped her where she wanted to go. It was all a rib."

"And what about Alderson?"

"She saw nothing of him, knows nothing about him."

"But he chased that car."

"I know. The girl says the blond fellow drove like a maniac for no reason other than the hell of it, so maybe Alderson never caught up with them."

"You believe that yarn?"

"I don't believe any story without satisfactory evidence in support. But hers casts grave doubt upon yours."

"All right. I know you're going to check on mine. Check on hers too and see if it stands up."

"We've already made a partial check on both of you and we're going to finish the job as soon as possible. The girl doesn't know the names of the three fellows or anything else about them other than what we've already got. She didn't notice the number of the car. Having suffered nothing, she had no reason to grab the number."

"That's a big help."

"But the rest looks convincing," said Ledsom. "She is a girl of excellent reputation coming from a highly respected family. She left home when she says she did, missed the bus she says she missed, was seen by two witnesses being offered a lift. She arrived at her destination at the time she states and can prove it."

"Those fellows took her a long way round?"

"Yes. They were feeling their oats."

"Nice way of accounting for lost time such as that involved in stopping, shooting, starting and running every mile of seventeen around a loop-road."

"Look, Mr. Harper, it's almost twenty-four hours since Alderson was shot down. All we've got are you and this girl. All I know is that somebody used a gun and somebody's telling lies."

"If that girl is telling the truth, which I beg leave to doubt," ventured Harper, "there's only one solution. A third party is wandering loose, untraced, unsuspected and laughing up his sleeve."

"There's not the slightest evidence of it." Ledsom hesitated, went on, "I wouldn't dream of chewing the fat with you in this manner if it wasn't that your hometown law gave you a very big hand. That sort of thing counts with me."

"I suppose so."

"Therefore I'll tell you something more. The three fellows don't tally with any trio released or escaped from prison this year."

"How about the military prisons? That old bird at the filling station thought they might be wearing altered uniforms."

"There is no military, naval or air force uniform corresponding with that description."

"Not in this country. Maybe they were foreigners."

"The girl says not. They spoke the language as only we can speak it and knew the country like the backs of their hands."

"Have you asked the authorities whether they know of *any* uniform that does correspond?"

"No. The girl agrees that their clothes had a sort of official look and thinks they were wearing army disposal stuff dyed green. If so, we've poor chance of tracing it. Ex-army jackets have been thrown on the market by the thousands."

"How about their car? You thought it might be stolen."

"To date we've pulled in reports of ten missing in various parts of the country. Four of them are green. We have urgent calls out for those four numbers. No luck so far." He gazed morbidly through an adjacent window. "Anyway, they may have resprayed it and changed the tags. Or it may be legitimately owned. Or it may be a rented car. The Thunderbug is a popular make. It would take months to check all sales and rentals from coast to coast."

Harper thought it over and said, "Well, you'll know it if ever you lay hands on it. You have a tyre-cast and that's something."

"Doesn't follow it's one of theirs. Anybody could have gone up that lane any time the same day. All we've discovered is that it doesn't belong to any logging vehicle. Neither do those three fellows answer the descriptions of any logging company's employees, past or present."

"No matter what that girl says, I still think they're the boys you want."

"The girl was an unwilling witness in that event. She wasn't a guilty party. So why should she cover up for a bunch of strangers?"

"Maybe they weren't strangers," Harper offered.

"What d'you mean?"

"Doesn't follow that because they gave her a lift they must have been unknown to her."

"She swears she didn't know them from Adam."

"You could bet on her saying that—if one of them happened to be a crazy boy-friend or a shiftless relative."

"H'm!" Ledsom viewed this as remotely possible but rather unlikely. He made a note on a pad. "Her local police gave us a report on her character, home conditions, status of parents and that's all. Might be worth probing more deeply into her background."

"If she's telling lies about a murder she must have a very strong reason. Perhaps she's been intimidated. Perhaps they have convinced her that they'll be back to cut her throat if she dares speak out of turn."

"Wrong guess," snapped Ledsom, positively. "I've been in this game a long time and I can tell when a suspect is secretly afraid. She wasn't. She was frankly bewildered at being dragged into something she didn't know a damn thing about."

"I'm a suspect too. A bigger and better one, to judge by what's happening right now. Think I'm scared?"

"No," admitted Ledsom.

"I ought to be—if I did it. But I didn't."

"Somebody did. We know that much." Ledsom studied him levelly. "I can hold you for twenty-four hours, and I'd do it if I'd a fair chance of pinning something on you by then. But it's going to take that long to empty the pond. So you can go. God help you if we salvage a gun traceable to you."

"I should worry."

Harper departed feeling distinctly surly, made the long drive home in ruminating silence. He passed at least fifty Thunderbugs in those seven hundred miles, saw no persons resembling the missing trio.

Chapter 3

He had a small plant employing six myopic but deft-fingered men. Also an office barely large enough to hold his desk and that of a secretary cum stenographer cum telephone operator. This person, name of Moira, was three inches taller than himself and about half the width. Cupid couldn't lug a ladder into the room and that fact suited Harper top-notch..

Sitting at his desk, he was examining a set of miniscule glass forceps under a powerful magnifier when Riley opened the door and took the two steps necessary to reach the middle. His plainclothes effectively advertised him as a cop in disguise.

"Morning, Lieutenant," greeted Harper, glancing up momentarily before returning attention to the task in hand.

"Morning, Neanderthal." There being no extra chair or space for one, Riley hooked a thick leg over a desk corner, rested himself as best he could. He bent forward to stare through the magnifier. "Beats me how paws so thick and hairy can fiddle with stuff that size."

"Why not? You pick your teeth, don't you?"

"Leave my personal habits out of this." His eyes became accusing. "Let's discuss some of yours."

Harper sighed, fitted the forceps into a velvet-lined case, placed it in a drawer. He shoved the magnifier to one side, looked up.

"Such as what?"

"Being around when things happen."

"Can I help it?"

"I don't know. Sometimes I wonder. It's mighty queer the way you latch on to this and that."

"Be specific," Harper invited.

"We've had a call. Fellow wants to know if you're still around. And if not, why not."

"All right, I'm still around. Go tell him."

"I wanted to know *why* he wanted to know," said Riley pointedly.

"And he told you. He said it isn't in the mud."

"Mud? What mud?"

"At the bottom of the pond." Harper grinned up at him. "He also asked whether I'm known to own a .32."

"You're right. It was Captain Ledsom. He gave me the details from first to last."

"Whereupon you solved the whole case for him," suggested Harper. "Two minds being better than one."

"*You* are going to solve it," said Riley.

"Am I?" Harper rubbed a chin and produced rasping noises. "Moira, throw this bum out."

"Do your own dirty work," ordered Riley. "You aren't paying her to act as bouncer as well, are you?" He turned to Moira. "How much are you making, Sylph?"

Moira giggled and said, "Not enough."

"Disgraceful," opined Riley, "I don't know why you stick with this hirsute curmudgeon."

"Such words," put in Harper. "I'll bet you can read too."

"And without moving my lips," Riley boasted. "So let's get down to basics. You're going to let business go to pot while you play Sherlock."

"Why?"

"Firstly because I told Ledsom you could clear up the matter if continuously kicked in the buttocks. So he wants me to kick."

"Secondly?"

"Because there's now a reward for information leading to apprehension and conviction of the killer or killers. Being human and in old shoes and wearing a tie obviously given with a gallon of alk, you could use the dough."

"That all?"

"Not by a long shot. I've saved the best bit to the last." He grinned, revealing big teeth. "An hour ago some hoarse-voiced character phoned Ledsom and said he'd seen Alderson having an argument with a compressed bruiser answering more or less to your description. Know what that makes you?"

"The sacrificial goat," said Harper moodily.

Riley nodded. "We'd pick you up and sweat a confession out of you but for two things. One is that we know you too well to believe you did it. The other is that the witness is not available to identify you."

"Why isn't he?"

"He said his piece and cut off. So Ledsom doesn't know who called."

"That looks fishy."

"Some folk hate to get involved," observed Riley. "More's the pity."

"I'm not surprised. I became too public-spirited myself. See what it's bought me."

"You jumped into it. Get busy and wriggle out of it."

"I can't afford the time," Harper complained.

"You can't afford a spell in clink either," Riley pointed out. "If Ledsom asks us to take you in we'll have to do it."

"Do you think that's likely?"

"God knows. It depends on what they turn up in the way of further evidence."

"If they find any pointing at me it will be purely circumstantial."

"That's a hell of a consolation when you're sitting around awaiting trial," said Riley. "The moment Ledsom believes he's got enough to convince a jury he'll make the pinch. He may then find he's wrong because the jury proves difficult to satisfy. So even if you get away with it you'll have been put through the mill, lost a lot of patience, time and money."

Harper said flatly, "They haven't the chance of a celluloid cat unless they find that witness and he identifies me. Even that won't be proof. It will do no more than suggest a motive. And if the witness does identify me he'll be a liar who knows something about the shooting and aims to divert attention. He can't appear without becoming a suspect himself."

"Could be. A way to find out would be to trace him and beat the truth out of him."

"The state troopers can do that themselves."

"Maybe," said Riley. "And maybe they couldn't."

"Maybe I couldn't either."

"I'm not so sure. You've done some darned funny things these last few years."

"Such as what?"

"That Grace Walterson murder. Twelve years old and unsolved—until you sit on a park bench and hear a boozy tramp muttering about it in his sleep. You tell us. We grab him and he confesses."

"Sheer luck," informed Harper.

"Was it? The Grace Walterson case had been long forgotten and wasn't in our bailiwick anyway. We had to check across country to get details. That guy did it all right. He was drunk like you said. There was only one respect in which his story didn't jibe with yours."

"What was that?"

"He didn't go to sleep and he didn't mutter. He swears he sat there blurry-eyed but wide-awake and wordless while you slid away and brought back a patrolman."

"He wrote his confession on paper and I ate it," said Harper. "I just can't resist paper." He frowned at the other. "You must be nuts. The sot voiced the burden on his conscience and gave himself away."

"All right." Riley stared at him very hard. "But *you* had to be there when he did it. Then there was the Tony Giacomo case. He heists a bank, kills two, and *you* have to be lounging near by two days later when he——"

"Oh, give it a rest," suggested Harper wearily. "I'm thirty-seven years old, have rubbed shoulders with nine wanted men and you pretend it's remarkable. How many have you sat next to in your half century of sin?"

"Plenty, I dare say. Not one of them told me he was wanted and begged me to take him in."

"None begged me, either."

"The entire bunch did the next best thing. They made the mistake of being someplace where you were too. You've upped our score of snatches by quite a piece and the Commissioner thinks you're Jesus. Smacks more of the Devil to me. There's something decidedly odd about it."

"Name it, then."

"I can't," confessed Riley. "I can't so much as imagine an explanation."

"Some folks are always there when accidents happen," Harper pointed out. "They can't help it. It's the way things go. Take my Aunt Matilda——"

"Let somebody else take her—I'm married," said Riley. "Are you going to break this case or do you prefer to squat on your fat tokus until I'm ordered to bring you in?"

"How much is the reward?"

Riley looked prayerfully at the ceiling. "He weakens at the thought of money. Five thousand dollars."

"I'll stew it awhile."

"If the idea is to wait for the reward to be jacked up," warned Riley, "you may wait too long. By the tone of his voice Ledsom's feeling mean enough to put his own mother in the jug."

With that, he bestowed a curt nod on Moira and walked out. They listened to his heavy footsteps parading along the outer passage and fading away in the distance.

"Moira, do you sense anything strange about me?"

"Oh no, Mr. Harper," she assured.

It was true enough. Her mind revealed that she wished he were ten inches taller and ten years younger. It might add a little spice to office work. She asked no more than that because her stronger emotional interests were being satisfied elsewhere.

He did not probe any more deeply into her thinking processes. His life resembled that of one perpetually walking by night through a city of well-lit and wide open bedrooms. He tried not to look, didn't want to look, but often could not avoid seeing. He was guilty of invasion of privacy twenty times per day, and just as frequently regretted it.

"Riley must be talking through his hat."

"Yes, Mr. Harper."

He called Riley on the phone mid-morning of the following day, announced, "You've given me the fidgets."

"That was my intention," said Riley, smirking in the tiny visiscreen.

"Everything is well in hand here, we being better organized than are some police headquarters. I reckon I can leave for a few days without risk of bankruptcy. But I'm not going away blind."

"What d'you mean?"

"For a start, I'll get nowhere if the moment I set foot across the line Ledsom's boys grab me for the hell of it."

"I'll 'tend to that," Riley promised. "They'll leave you alone—unless they can prove you're ready for cooking."

"I want the addresses of Alderson's widow and of that girl. Also of the fellow who phoned Ledsom—if they've managed to trace him."

"Leave it with me. I'll call you back as soon as I can."

Harper pronged the phone, watched its fluorescent dial cloud over and go blank. He did not like the situation. He felt no real concern over entanglement in a murder. That affair would straighten itself out sooner or later. It was the least of his worries.

What bothered him was the hulking but agile-minded Riley's vague suspicions concerning his aptitude for uncovering evil long hidden from everyone else. Though devoid of a satisfactory theory to explain it, Riley had him tagged as a natural born smeller-out of witches.

The trick was easy enough. He had found out long ago that if he stared too long at a man with a guilty conscience the recipient of the stare became wary while the guilt radiated from his mind in vivid details. Nine times in the last ten years he had gazed absently at people who had rung a mental alarm-bell and unknowingly broadcast their reason for doing so. They had literally thought themselves into jail or the chair.

Harper had no difficulty in imagining the reaction should the news ever get out that no individual's mind was truly his own. He would be left without a friend other than some person of his own peculiar type, if such a one existed.

As for the criminal element, they'd see to it that his life wasn't worth a moment's purchase. The world's pleasantness so long preserved by his self-concealment would change to a hell of avoidance by day and menace by night.

While waiting for Riley, he indulged macabre amusement by picturing the manner of his own demise at the hands of the fearful. Obviously they couldn't use the conventional method of the gunman lurking in an alley. Such an assassin could not ready himself without thinking about the task in hand and thus warning the victim of the impending deed. No tactic could be effective that involved the presence of an active mind.

They would have to turn to some delayed or remotely controlled device that could function without radiating its intentions. A time-bomb might be suitable.

So he'd come to the office one morning, give Moira the cheery hiho, sit at his desk, pull open a drawer and—*bam*! Then the smoke would clear away and give him a view of the after life, if any.

Possibly he had been followed-up in police thought as a direct result of his foolishness in passing them news so openly and so often. He had been impelled to do it mostly because he detested finding himself in the presence of somebody who had got away with mayhem and any time might try to get away with it again. It irked his sense of justice. And it gratified him to feel that at long last some hapless victim had been avenged.

One fellow he had detected, chased and finally shot down had been seven times guilty of rape and once of murder accompanied by criminal assault. He could not let a louse like that freely run around for the sake of keeping Riley at arm's length.

In future it might be better to pass the word to the police by some indirect method such as, for example, the anonymous telephone call. It was doubtful whether that would serve. He had become too well-known a local character to leave the police puzzling over the source of the tip-offs. Any one of them, from the Commissioner downward, could put two and two together and make it four.

The phone yelped and Riley came on. "I've got those two addresses." He read them out while Harper made a note of them, then said, "The unknown caller hasn't been traced but Ledsom now thinks there's nothing to his message. They've found a fellow roughly corresponding to your description who gave Alderson some lip in the mid-morning. There were several witnesses and the caller in all probability was one of those."

"What was this squabbler doing at 4 p.m.?"

"He's in the clear. He was miles away and can prove it."

"H'm! All right, I'll go take a look around and hope my luck holds out."

"*Is* it luck?" asked Riley pointedly.

"Bad luck, to my way of thinking," said Harper. "If you had fathered ten sets of twins you'd appreciate without being told that some men can be afflicted."

"More likely I'd appreciate that some guys know how," Riley retorted. "And that's the trouble with you—so go to it!"

He faded off the screen. Harper sighed for the third time, tucked the slip of paper with its addresses into a vest pocket, spoke to Moira.

"I'll phone each day to see what's doing. If you can't handle something urgent and important you'll have to nurse it until I ring through."

"Yes, Mr. Harper."

"And if anyone turns up to pinch me tell them they're too late—I'm on the lam."

"Oh, Mr. Harper!"

Ruth Alderson proved to be a pretty blond with sad eyes. Obviously she was still in much of a mental whirl.

Sitting opposite her and idly turning his hat in his hands, Harper said, "I hate to trouble you at such a time, Mrs. Alderson, but it is necessary. I have a special interest in this case. I found your husband and was the last to speak to him."

"Did he——?" She swallowed hard, stared at him pathetically. "Did he . . . suffer much?"

"It was all very quick. He was too dazed to feel pain. He talked of you then kind of faded away. Betty, he said, Betty. Then he was gone." He frowned in puzzlement, added, "But your name is Ruth."

"He always called me Betty. Said it suited me. He made a pet name of it."

She put on a sudden tearfulness, covered her face with her hands, made no sound. He watched her quietly awhile.

When she had recovered, he said, "There's a slight chance you might be able to help find the rat who did it."

"How?"

"Tell me, did Bob have any enemies?"

She considered the question, gathering her thoughts with difficulty. "He arrested a number of people. Some went to jail. I don't suppose they loved him for that."

"Did any of them promise to get him when they came out?"

"If they did, he never mentioned it to me. It isn't the sort of thing he would tell." She paused, went on, "Four years ago he caught a man named Josef Grundoff and Bob said that when he was sentenced Grundoff swore to kill the judge."

"But he did not threaten your husband?"

"Not to my knowledge."

"You cannot recall any occasion on which somebody has menaced your husband specifically?"

"No, I can't."

"Nor any time when extraordinary resentment has been shown as a result of his doing his duty?"

"He had wordy arguments twice a week," she said wearily. "He often came home riled about someone. But as far as I can tell it was the normal give and take between the police and the public. I know of nobody who hated him enough to kill him."

"Only this Grundoff?"

"Grundoff only threatened the judge."

"I don't like pestering you this way, Mrs. Alderson, but can you recall any incident that seemed to worry your husband, even if only temporarily? Any small happening, no matter how insignificant, at any time in the past?"

"Not in connection with his police duties," she replied. A faint smile came into her features. "All his bothers were domestic ones. He was a bag of nerves when my babies were due."

Harper nodded understanding, continued with, "One more angle. It is imperative that I try it. Please forgive me, won't you?"

"What do you mean?" Her eyes widened.

"You are an attractive person, Mrs. Alderson. Did Bob earn anyone's enmity by marrying you?"

She flushed and gave back strongly, "The idea is quite ridiculous."

"Not at all. Such things have happened. They will happen again and again. Jealousy is perhaps the oldest motive for murder. It feeds upon itself, unseen, unsuspected. You might well have been admired and desired without realizing it."

"I don't think so."

"Since your marriage has any male friend or acquaintance shown undue attention toward you or displayed more than average friendship?" He saw the revulsion rising in her mind, knew that he could have expressed himself more tactfully, added with haste, "I do not expect you to be aware of an unconfessed lover. I am asking you to help seek a possible killer."

She cooled down, said dully. "There is nobody."

"When you first met Bob did you leave anybody for his sake?"

"I did not. I was free and unattached."

"Thank you, Mrs. Alderson." He stood up, glad to be at the end of the matter. "I apologize most sincerely for subjecting you to all this. And I really do appreciate your co-operation." He followed her to the front door, paused there, patted her gently on the shoulder. "Nothing anyone can say is adequate. Actions speak louder than words. You have my card. Any time I can help, please call on me to do so. I shall consider it a privilege."

"You are very kind," she murmured.

He got into his car, watched her close the door, said to himself savagely, "Damn! Damn!"

A mile down the road he stopped beside a phone booth and called Ledsom.

"So it's you," said the police captain, not visibly over-joyed. "What d'you want this time?"

"Some information."

"About what?"

"A character named Josef Grundoff."

"You're doing fine, digging up that hoodlum," Ledsom commented. "I wouldn't have thought of him myself."

"Why not?"

"He got twenty years for second degree murder. It will be a long, long time before he's out."

"Is that all?" asked Harper.

"How much more do you want?"

"Official reassurance that he's still inside. Maybe he has escaped."

"We'd have been advised of it. They'd send out fliers within twenty-four hours."

"Do you think it worth checking?" Harper persisted. "Just in case some notice has gone astray?"

"I can do that in five minutes," Ledsom became crabbed and demanded, "How did you get hold of Grundoff's name, anyway?"

"From Mrs. Alderson."

The other registered surprise. "Surely she hasn't told you that Grundoff——?"

"She said only that he'd sworn to get the judge," Harper chipped in. "So it seemed to me possible that he might have had Alderson's name on his list as well."

"He had no list. He was merely making tough talk. The judge said twenty years and Grundoff went nuts. That sort of thing happens often." He was silent a moment then continued, "I'll check all the same. It's one chance in a million but we can't overlook it. Call me back a bit later."

Harper phoned him from a diner twenty miles farther on.

"No luck," Ledsom informed. "Grundoff is still in the jug."

"Did he have any pals who might do his dirty work for him?"

"No. He was a lone wolf."

"Do you think he may have made friends in clink who've been released and started tending his affairs?"

"Not on your life," scoffed Ledsom. "No ex-con is going to shoot up a cop merely to please some leg still inside. There would have to be money in it, big money. Grundoff couldn't dig up ten bucks."

"Thanks," said Harper glumly. "So that's another wrong tree up which I've barked. Oh well, press on regardless."

"To where?"

"That girl who was in the Thunderbug. Did you learn any more about her?"

"Yes. Her boy friend is in the armed forces and serving overseas. She has no relative with a police record, no bad egg in the family. Helps us a lot, doesn't it?"

"How about her protecting a girl friend who, perhaps, is afflicted with a trigger-happy lover?"

"How about pigs taking wings? The follow-up has been good and thorough. Her entire circle of relatives, neighbours and friends is in the clear."

"All right, keep your hair on. I'm only a major suspect trying to establish my pristine purity."

Ledsom let go a loud snort and cut off. Evidently lack of progress was trying his patience.

* * *

The second address was that of the central house in an old-fashioned but still imposing terrace of substantially built property. The road was wide, quiet, tree-lined and had an air of stuffy respectability. Harper went up six steps, thumbed the bell-stud.

A tall, good-looking youth of about eighteen answered the door, eyed him quizzically.

"Miss Jocelyn Whittingham in?" Harper asked, trying to sound official or at least semi-official.

"No." The other's mind confirmed the truth of that but went on to whisper to itself, *"Joyce doesn't want to see anybody. Who is this muscle-bound ape? Another nosey cop? Or a reporter? Joyce is fed up answering questions. Why don't they leave her alone?"*

"Any idea when she'll be back?"

"No."

That was a lie. The girl had promised to return by six.

"H'm!" Harper glanced up and down the road in the manner of one idly wondering what to do next. In deceptively casual tones he tried to hand the other a mental wallop. "Ever plugged a state trooper?"

No alarm-bell rang in the opposing brain. The youth's thoughts swirled confusedly while he doubted his own ears.

"Have I ever *what*?"

"Sorry," said Harper, knowing his blow had gone wide of the mark. "I was thinking out loud about something else. When do you suppose I could see Miss Whittingham?"

"I don't know."

Same lie again.

"Too bad." Harper registered indecision.

"What d'you want to see her about?" inquired the youth.

"A personal matter."

"Well, she isn't in, and I don't know when she'll be in."

"Suppose I call back between six and seven?"

"Please yourself." He showed facial indifference while

43

his mind nursed the notion that the visitor could go jump in the lake.

"All right, I'll try again later."

The youth nodded, shut the door. He was not sufficiently interested even to ask Harper's name. He was devoid of guilt and bored by the affairs of his sister, Miss Jocelyn Whittingham.

Harper spent an hour strolling aimlessly around the town while his car was greased and serviced in a central garage. At twenty to six he returned on foot to the road, stationed himself by a bus stop fifty yards from the house, kept watch for the girl's homecoming.

He had only a rough description of his quarry, but needed no more than that. One question would serve to stimulate self-identification voluntarily or involuntarily. There is no way of preventing the brain from registering its negatives or affirmatives no matter how great the desire to distort it.

Once the girl got inside that house the puzzle then would be how to gain an interview contrary to her wishes. If she flatly refused to see him he had no power to compel her to do so. In such circumstances his only positive tactic would be to cajole the local police into bringing her in for further questioning. They would not do that without excellent reason, and it was distasteful to him to invent a reason.

A face-to-face interview was imperative. If she were indoors he could stand there all night picking up her thoughts and sorting them out from other nearby thoughts with no difficulty whatsoever. He could, if he wished, spy upon her mind for a week.

It would do him not the slightest bit of good so long as her mind and its thinking processes moved only in channels having nothing to do with the case in hand. Questions were necessary to force her brain on to the case and make it reveal any cogent evidence it might be hiding. A vocal stimulus was required. To provide it he must ask her about this and that, drawing useful conclusions from all points where her thoughts contradicted her words.

Twice while he waited a girl walked past and momentarily captured his attention. So long as they did not mount the steps to the house he made no attempt to identify them mentally. He had his code of ethics developed since early childhood; he did not listen to private musings except when circumstances impelled him to do so. Of course, he could not avoid hearing the sudden cry of an alarmed conscience or a loud call for help such as Alderson had broadcast. But the muted voice of a passing mind, lacking the amplitude of defensive untruths, went by him unheard. He merely watched those girls until they had gone beyond the house and departed from sight.

A few minutes later a third girl came from the farther end of the road. She, too, ignored the house, continued straight on and rounded the far corner. A bus pulled up at the stop, discharged four passengers and rolled away. One of them, a tall, sallow man, eyed him curiously.

"It'll be half an hour before there's another."

"Yes, I know."

The other shrugged, crossed the road, entered the house facing the stop. Harper moved some distance down the road where he could keep watch without being snooped upon from the windows by the sallow man.

At five to six a girl entered the road from the end nearest his former post, walked hurriedly along with a sharp click-click of high heels. She was of medium height, fresh-featured, plump and about twenty. Without glancing around or noticing Harper, she climbed the steps to the house, felt in her handbag for a key.

From seventy yards away Harper probed at her, seeking confirmation of her identity. The result was shocking. The precise instant his mind touched hers she became aware of the contact and he, in his turn, knew that she was aware.

She dropped the handbag in her flurry, bent and grabbed for it as he started to run toward her.

Getting the bag, she fumbled inside it with frantic haste while his feet pounded heavily along the sidewalk. Her eyes held a luminous glare as she found the key, stabbed it at the door. Perspiration beaded the running Harper's broad features while his right hand pawed under his left arm and his legs continued to race.

The key slid in and turned. Harper stopped at ten yards distance, levelled his gun and squeezed its butt. The thing went *spat-spat-spat* with such swiftness that it sounded like somebody tearing a foot of canvas. The noise was not loud. A stream of matchhead sized steel balls hit the target dead centre.

Miss Jocelyn Whittingham let go the key, sank to her knees without a sound, keeled over with her head against the door. Harper stood sweating, watched the blood run out of her hair and listened to her brain packing up for keeps.

He stared around, saw no onlookers, no witnesses. The brief plinking of gunfire had attracted nobody's attention. He left her lying there and paced swiftly up the road. His face was strained and wet as he retrieved his car and got out of town fast.

Chapter 4

The police must have moved fast and skilfully. He had covered a mere three hundred miles before he was advertised on the air and in the news-sheets. He was having supper in a cheap hashery when he got an evening paper carrying the news.

WANTED FOR MURDER, it said. There followed a fairly accurate description of himself and of his car, complete with tag number. He cursed underbreath as he read it. There were twenty customers in the place, most of them long-distance truckers. Half of them had read or were reading the same sheet. Some were unaware of his existence; the others glanced at him casually and without suspecting that the subject of the report was here under their very eyes. He knew their lack of suspicion with absolute certainty and that was about the only advantage he possessed.

Outside, in plain view, stood the car. Its numbers seemed to swell and grow enormous even as he looked at them. Three big men in denims lumbered past its rear end without giving it so much as a second look, got into an adjacent machine and pulled away. His luck might hold out like that for some time but it just couldn't last for ever. Sooner or later the number-plate would be spotted waiting somewhere, by somebody with sharp eyes and a good memory.

He could leave the car where it was and help himself to another. When you're wanted for murder a mere theft can't add to the grief. But to do that would have compensating disadvantages. The number of the stolen car would be broadcast in short time, leaving him no better off than before. Moreover, right now the law did not know whether he was heading for Peking or Pernambuco but a car-swap would give away the direction of his escape and get every hick deputy on the lookout for him ahead. Also it would reveal that he had crossed state lines to evade arrest, a federal offence that might bring in the F.B.I.

The F.B.I. needed bringing in. Of that he was more than positive. But he did not relish the notion of the F.B.I. taking part in a nation-wide hunt for himself, especially since someone over-excitable might copy his recent tactic by shooting first and asking questions afterward. He was in the most peculiar position of wanting to get to the F.B.I. before they could get to him.

The means by which the law had tagged him as the culprit could be guessed quite easily. Ledsom's knowledge that he was visiting the girl. Her brother's description of the caller at the door. The sallow man's evidence about the lounger at the bus stop. Above all, the missiles in the body, like unto bullets from no other gun.

Stewing it over, he could not help wondering whether Ledsom now felt certain that he knew who had killed Alderson. It would be a very natural tendency on that officer's part to assume the same hand in both cases even though different weapons had been used.

What he liked least about this sudden howl for a man named Harper was not that it boosted the official hunt for him, but that it might start an unofficial search. The forces of law and order should not be the only ones to take deep interest in the datum that he had killed Miss Jocelyn Whittingham. Certain others undoubtedly would be after him, anxious to know how it all came about, anxious to deal with him before it was too late. Those three fellows in the Thunderbug, for instance.

Swallowing the rest of his coffee, he got out of the place as quickly as he could without drawing attention to his urgency. He waited nervily by a row of alk-pumps while his tank was filled, then drove at top pace into the twilight that rapidly became night, a dark, moonless night. He had more than five hundred miles yet to go.

At four-forty in the morning, with the pale halo of dawn beginning to show in the east, some wide-awake sharp-eye either read his plates or chased him on general principles.

He reached a half-mile stretch of road under repair, perforce crawled at fifteen over the torn surface. A watchman's hut stood at the end, and beside it a car with side-lamps glowing. He passed the hut, accelerated, gained speed and a mile and a half lead when the parked car came to life, shot out on to the road, went after him with spotlight blinking.

Harper could not hear a siren nor pick up following thoughts. He was too far ahead and too preoccupied with driving. He shoved the pedal down to the floorboards and let the machine leap ahead. If the pursuers were police, as their spotlight suggested, that alone would be enough to convince them that they were on to something worth running down.

There was no alternative other than letting them chase. If he was going to be taken in it must be by people who were peculiarly well informed and knew how many beans make five. He was pretty certain that no county sheriff, no state, city or town police possessed the information that qualified them to become his captors.

49

Tyres squealed, headlights swung and rocked as he took a couple of bends at breakneck speed. The car was powerful and fast, in tiptop condition, but the one behind might be even better. So far as he could judge from frequent glances at the rear-view mirror, the other machine did have a slight advantage because its winking spotlight seemed to be creeping up on him ever so gradually.

With his needle trembling at over ninety he tore through a crossroads, along a main artery darkened still more by large trees on both sides. The trees whizzed past like huge ghosts, arms out, transfixed by this night-time pursuit.

There was no traffic other than his own car and the one behind. Far ahead and slightly to his right he could see the sky-glow from street lights of a sizeable city, wondered whether he could make it that distance and, if so, what he'd do when he got there. Maybe if the ones behind came close enough in the next ten miles they'd start shooting. What to do then?

He rocked around another half-bend, momentarily lost the lights in the mirror which by now were less than a mile to the rear. His own beams swung briefly across the end of a track through thick timber. He dived into it so suddenly and recklessly that for a second or two he feared the machine would overturn.

Switching off all lamps he ploughed another fifty yards into complete blackness, meanwhile praying that he would not hit an invisible tree or dive into a hidden ditch. Twigs crackled and snapped under rolling wheels but luck remained with him. He braked, dropped a window, watched and listened.

The siren could be heard now. A prowl car, sure enough. By this time it was on top of the bend. Headlights slewed across the night as it came round and the next moment it thundered past, wailing as it went. Its passing was far too swift to enable Harper to see how many were within or to pick up a random thought.

50

He sat in darkness until he could see faint, diminished beams racing up a slope four miles away. Then he reversed, got back on to the road, made off in the way he had come. Reaching the cross-roads over which he had recently blundered, he turned to the right, continued along this new route.

Without further incident he reached Washington late in the morning, planted the car in a park on the outskirts, took a bus into the city. There he found a phone and called the office.

Either the office visiscreen was out of order or had been switched off, for his own screen remained blank and Moira's response was equally blank.

"Harper plant. Can I help you?"

"Only God can help me," he said. "This is your boss."

She let out a distinct gasp.

"What's so soul-shaking about that?" he demanded. "You have spoken to me many a time before."

"Yes, Mr. Harper. Of course, Mr. Harper." She sought desperately for words. "I didn't expect you just yet."

"Tsk!" He grinned wolfishly at the dead screen. "Why not? I told you I'd call, didn't I?"

"Certainly, Mr. Harper, but——"

"But *what*?"

She hadn't the vaguest idea what. She was tongue-tied and in a tangle.

"You've been reading the papers," he observed grimly. "But no matter. Has anything turned up?"

"Turned up?"

"Look, Moira, pay no attention to those fat-butted dicks sitting on my desk. Listen to me: has anything come along in the mail that requires my personal handling?"

"N-n-no, Mr. Harper."

"Any complications I'm needed to clear up?"

"N-n-no."

"All right. Put one of those guys on the phone."

51

She got into a worse tangle. "I don't understand, Mr. Harper. There isn't——"

"Now, now, no lies!" he ordered.

At that point she gave up and he heard her say weakly to somebody else, "He knows you're here and insists on speaking to you."

There sounded a deep grunt that somehow conveyed disgust. Harper's screen suddenly cleared and showed a beefy face scowling at him.

Before the other could speak Harper said, "When I can't see a thing in my own office I know somebody doesn't want me to look. I also know Moira's been told to keep me on as long as she can while this call is being traced. Well, you're wasting your time for which suffering taxpayers are paying, of whom I am one. You pack up and get busy on the local sinners. Tell Riley I love him despite all his faults."

The face scowled more deeply. "Now see here, Harper——"

"Listen to me for once," continued Harper impatiently. "It may help persuade you that you're doing no good warming my blotter if I tell you I'm calling from Washington and that I'm making for F.B.I headquarters to give myself up."

Incredulity expressed itself on the distant features. "You mean that?"

"Check with the F.B.I. in about fifteen minutes' time. They'll tell you they've got me. And don't celebrate by pawing Moira around. She draws her pay from me, not from you!"

He pronged the phone and walked out, joined the crowds on the sidewalk. He had covered two blocks when a tall, dark-haired, neatly dressed young man threw him a brief but penetrating glance in passing, did a swift double-take, continued a few yards beyond then turned and followed.

Harper strolled steadily on, smiling to himself as he filched data out of the shadower's mind. Robert Slade, thirty-two, F.B.I. agent, obsessed by the notion that Harper bore a very close resemblance to Harper. The encounter was purely accidental but the boy intended to stick to the opportunity until he was sure enough to make a pinch.

Turning down a side street, Harper covered three more blocks, became a mite uncertain of his whereabouts. He was not very familiar with Washington. He stopped on a corner, lit a cigarette, gazed furtively over cupped hands, found Slade studiously examining a window full of panes-in-the-neck.

Ambling back he touched Slade's elbow, said, "Pardon me. I'm looking for F.B.I. headquarters. Can you direct me?"

It shook Slade more than if he'd suddenly stuck a gun in his belly.

"Why...er...yes, of course." His clear grey eyes betrayed uncertainty about his suspicions. His mind was saying, "Hell of a coincidence!"

"You're Robert Slade, aren't you?" inquired Harper, pleasantly conversational.

The other rocked back. "I am. You have the advantage of me, though. I don't recall knowing you."

"Would it do you any good to make an arrest?"

"What d'you mean?"

"I'm seeking your H.Q. You can show me the way. If you would like to call it a pinch it's all right with me. I'm Wade Harper."

Slade took in a deep breath. "You're not kidding?"

"Why should I? Don't I look like Harper?"

"You sure do. And maybe you're fed up being mistaken for him. If so, there's little we can do about it."

"That can soon be settled. You have my prints on file." He felt under an arm. "Here's my gun. Don't let the comparison boys in the ballistics department lose it—I hope to get it back someday."

"Thanks." Openly baffled, Slade shoved it into a pocket, pointed down the street. "This way."

They moved along side by side. Slade made no suggestion of using his handcuffs, neither was he particularly wary. Harper's attitude had created within him a condition of chronic scepticism; he was inclined to think this capture would gain him no kudos because the captive was too self-possessed to be other than innocent.

Reaching the big building they went inside. Slade showed Harper into a small room, said, "Wait there a minute," and departed. The exit and the open street were within easy reach. There was no obstacle to an escape other than that provided by a hard-looking character on duty at the door.

Taking his ease in a pneumatic chair Harper amused himself tracking Slade's mind. The agent went along a short corridor, entered an office, spoke to somebody there.

"*I've just picked up Wade Harper. He's in room number four.*"

"*By himself?*"

"*Yes.*"

"*Are you cracked? He can make a dive and——*"

"*He was on his way here when I found him,*" interjected Slade, honestly refusing the credit for the grab. "*He wanted to come.*"

"*Holy smoke! There's something mighty funny about this.*" A pause, then, "*Bring him in here.*"

Harper got up, walked along the passage, arrived at the door just as Slade opened it to come and get him. For the third successive time Slade was taken aback. He stood aside, silent and puzzled, while Harper marched boldly in, took a seat and gazed at the lean-faced man behind the desk. The latter returned his gaze and gave himself away without knowing it. William Pritchard, thirty-nine, area supervisor.

"Morning, Mr. Pritchard," said Harper with the cheerful air of one who has not a worry in the world.

Pritchard blinked, marshalled his wits, said, "There's a

call out for you. You're wanted for the murder of Jocelyn Whittingham."

"Yes, I know. I read the papers."

"Somebody's blundered," thought Pritchard, impressed by this coolness. *"He's got an alibi."* Clearing his throat, he asked, "Well, do you wish to say anything about it?"

"Plenty—but not to you."

"Why not to me?"

"No personal reason, I assure you. I'd like to talk to Sam Stevens."

"Go see where he is," Pritchard ordered after a little hesitation, deciding that one interlocutor was as good as another.

Slade went away, came back, informed, "Stevens is in Seattle."

The phone called shrilly, Pritchard picked it off his desk, said, "Yes? How did you know? Oh, he told you himself, did he? No, he wasn't fooling. He's here all right. He's in front of me right now." He racked the phone, stared hard at Harper. "You can't see Stevens. He isn't available."

"A pity. He could have got me somebody high up. I want to talk as high as I can get."

"Why?"

"I refuse to say."

Frowning disapproval, Pritchard leaned forward. "Did you or did you not shoot this Whittingham girl?"

"Yes, I did."

"All right. Are you willing to sign a confession to that effect?"

"No."

"You admit shooting her but you refuse to sign a confession?"

"That's right."

"Care to offer a reason?" Pritchard invited, studying him carefully.

"I've a good reason. I didn't kill her."

"But she's dead. She's as dead as mutton. Didn't you know that?"

Harper made two waves of a hand in manner suggesting that this was a minor point of little consequence.

"So you shot her but didn't kill her?" Pritchard persisted. "You put a dozen steel beads through her skull but somehow refrained from committing homicide?"

"Correct."

That did it. Pritchard's and Slade's minds worked in perfect accord, weighed the evidence, reached a simultaneous verdict: not guilty of murder by reason of insanity.

Sighing deeply, Harper said, "Sam Stevens is the only boy I know in this outfit. He made a check on my plant once, about two years ago. He entered it on some sort of national security list which you people keep on file. He gave me a gun-permit and a bunch of bureaucratic instructions chief of which says I'm federal property the moment war breaks out. I become confiscated lock, stock and barrel."

"So?" prompted Pritchard, seeing no point in this.

"The Whittingham business has to do more or less with the same issue, namely, national security. Therefore I can talk only to somebody who'll know what I'm talking about."

"That would be Jameson," promptly whispered Pritchard's thoughts.

"Such as Jameson," Harper added.

They reacted as though he had uttered a holy name in the unholy precincts of a cheap saloon.

"Or whoever is *his* boss," said Harper, for good measure.

With a touch of severity, Pritchard demanded, "You just said that Stevens is the only member of the F.B.I. known to you. So how do you know of Jameson? Come to that, how did you know *my* name?"

"He knew mine too," put in Slade, openly itching for a plausible explanation.

"That's a problem I'll solve only in the presence of somebody way up top," said Harper. He smiled at Pritchard and inquired, "How's your body?"

"Eh?"

Out of the other's bafflement Harper extracted a clear and detailed picture of the body, said in helpful tones, "You have a fish-shaped birthmark on the inside of your left thigh."

"That's enough for me!" Pritchard stood up, badly worried. He said to Slade, "You keep an eye on this Houdini while I go see what Jameson says." He departed hurriedly.

Harper asked Slade, "May I have a sheet of paper, please?"

Extracting one from a drawer in the desk Slade slipped it across. He watched Harper take out a fountain-pen and prepare to write. The confession after all, he thought. Definitely a nut who'd refuse a thing one moment and give it the next. Strange how even an intelligent man could go so completely off his rocker. An hereditary weakness, perhaps.

Ignoring these uncomplimentary ideas which assailed him as clearly as if they'd been shouted aloud, Harper waited a few moments then began to write. He scribbled with great rapidity, finished a short time before Pritchard's return.

"He won't see you," announced Pritchard with a that-is-that air.

"I know." Harper gave him the paper.

Glancing over it, Pritchard popped his eyes, ran out full tilt. Slade stared after him, turning a questioning gaze upon Harper.

"That was a complete and accurate transcript of their conversation," Harper informed. "Want to lay any bets against him seeing me now?"

"No," said Slade, developing the willies. "I don't care to throw away good money."

Jameson proved to be a middle-aged bull of a man with a thick mop of curly grey hair. His eyes were blue and cold, his manner that of one long accustomed to the exercising of authority. Sitting erect in his chair he kept one strong forefinger firmly planted on the sheet of paper lying on the desk before him. He wasted no time in getting down to business.

"How did you do it?"

"Easily enough. I took aim, fired and down she slid."

"I'm not asking about that." The finger tapped impatiently. "I am referring to this."

"Oh, the eavesdropping." Harper pretended to gain an understanding that he had not lost in the first place. "I did it in the same way the enemy might be able to do it any time he wants to know what we're up to."

"You may go," Jameson said to Pritchard. "I'll call you when I want you." He waited until the door had closed, fixed full attention on the other. "Are you categorically asserting that agents of other powers are able to read our minds at will?"

"No."

"Then why make such a suggestion?"

"I'm merely putting over the theory that what one can do another can do," said Harper. "It's a notion I've nursed for years. So far I've been unable to find any evidence in support."

"Obviously you are talking about something *you* can do. What can you do?"

"That," said Harper, pointing to the paper.

Jameson was no fool. He had got the idea at the start but found considerable difficulty in absorbing it. The manifest explanation was proving indigestible. He tried again to cope with it, failed, decided to put the issue fairly and squarely.

"It would take a telepath to play these sort of tricks."

"Nothing else but," agreed Harper.

"Whoever heard of one?" asked Jameson, battling his own incredulity.

Harper merely shrugged.

Switching his little intercom-board, Jameson spoke into its mike. "Is Miss Keyes there? Put her on. Miss Keyes, I want you to type a column of twenty-eight-digit numbers chosen at random. Bring it to me immediately you have finished." He switched off, gave Harper a challenging look, poked the paper toward him and said, "See what you can do with that."

"Now I've got to search through the general mess for somebody concocting meaningless numbers," Harper complained. "I may miss the first one or two while I'm feeling around."

"Never mind. Do the best you can. If you get only a quarter of them it will convince me that the age of miracles has not passed."

Harper wrote down eighteen of them plus the last two digits of the nineteenth. Taking the paper without comment, Jameson waited for Miss Keyes. She arrived shortly, gave him her list, departed with no visible surprise. If she'd been ordered to wear her machine's dust-cover as a hat she would have done it without question. Jameson compared the two columns.

Finally he said, "This is worse than a bomb in the Pentagon. Nothing is private property any more."

"I know."

"How did it happen?"

"Can a man with a hare-lip tell you how it happened? All I know is that I was born that way. For a few years I assumed that everyone else was precisely like myself. Being a child it took quite a time to learn that it was not so, to learn that I was a one-eyed man in the kingdom of the blind, to learn that I could be feared and that the feared are hated."

"There must be a reason for it," said Jameson.

"Does it matter?"

"It matters a hell of a lot. You are a freak created by some very special arrangement of circumstances. If we could detail those circumstances fully and completely we could

59

estimate the likelihood of them being duplicated elsewhere. That in turn would give us a fair idea of whether there are any more like you and, if so, who's got them."

Harper said quietly and soberly, "I don't think that matters a damn either. Not any more."

"Why doesn't it?"

"Because I made mental contact with Jocelyn Whittingham and she promptly called me an insulting name. So I shot her."

"You considered that adequate motive for murder?" prompted Jameson.

"In view of the name, yes!"

"What did she call you?"

"A terrestrial bastard," informed Harper, hard-eyed.

Chapter 5

For a full two minutes Jameson sat there like one paralysed. His thoughts milled wildly around and he was momentarily oblivious of the fact that the other could read them as easily as if they shone in neons.

Then he asked, "Are you sure of that?"

"The only person in the world who can be positive about someone else's mind is a telepath," assured Harper. "I'll tell you something else: I shot her because I knew I couldn't kill her. It was a physical impossibility."

"How d'you make that out?"

"No living man could harm Jocelyn Whittingham— because she was already dead."

"Now see here, we have a detailed police report——"

"I killed something else," said Harper, with devastating effect. "The thing that had already slaughtered her."

Jameson promptly went into another whirl. He had a cool, incisive mind used to dealing with highly complicated but essentially normal problems. This was the first time

61

within his considerable experience that he had been slapped in the face by a sample of the supernormal. Even now he strove to cope with it in rational, everyday terms. It was about as easy as trying to use a yardstick to measure the distance to the Moon.

One thing surprised the observing Harper, namely, that much of the other's confusion stemmed from the fact that he lacked certain information he could reasonably be expected to possess. High up in the bureaucratic hierarchy Jameson might be, evidently he was not high enough. All the same, he had enough pull to take the matter further and get some action.

Harper said, "You've got the bald account from police sources. It isn't enough. I'd like to give you my side of the story."

"Go ahead," invited Jameson, glad to concentrate on something that might clear up the muddle.

Commencing with his pick-up of the dying Alderson's broadcast, Harper took it through to the end.

Then he said, "No ordinary human being is ever aware of his mind being read. He gains no sense of physical contact that might serve to warn him. He remains completely unconscious of being pried into. I have been absorbing your thoughts the whole time we've been here together; your senses have not registered the probe in any way whatever, have they?"

"No," Jameson admitted.

"And if I had not told you that I'm a telepath, and satisfied you as to the truth of it, you'd have found no cause to suspect that your mind is wide open to me, would you?"

"No."

"Well," went on Harper reminiscently, "the instant I touched the mind inside Jocelyn Whittingham it felt the contact, knew whence it came, took wild alarm and hated me with a most appalling ferocity. In the same instant I detected all its reactions and recognized it as non-human.

The contact did not last a fiftieth of a second but it was enough. I knew it as nothing born of woman. I knew it as surely as your own eyes can tell you that a rattlesnake is not a mewling babe."

"If it wasn't human," inquired Jameson, with much scepticism, "what was it?"

"That I don't know."

"Of what shape or form?"

"The shape and form of the Whittingham girl. It *had* to be that. It was using her body."

Disbelief suddenly swamped Jameson's brain. "I will concede that you are either a genuine telepath or the practitioner of some new and superb trick that makes you look like one. But that doesn't mean I have to swallow this murder story. What your defence boils down to is that you shot a corpse animated by God knows what. No jury on earth will give such an incredible plea a moment's consideration."

"I'll never face a jury," Harper told him.

"I think you will—unless you drop dead beforehand. The law must take its course."

"For the first time in my naughty life I'm above the law," said Harper, impressively confident. "What's more, the law itself is going to say so."

"How do you reach that remarkable conclusion?"

"The law isn't interested only in the death of Jocelyn Whittingham. It is even more concerned about the slaying of Trooper Alderson, he having been a police officer. And you can't pin *that* one on me if you try from now to Christmas. Reason why you can't is because I didn't do it."

"Then who did?" Jameson challenged.

"A-a-ah!" Harper eyed him meaningfully. "Now you're getting right down to the heart of the matter. Who killed Alderson and why?"

"Well?"

"Three men in a Thunderbug. Three men who, in all

probability, resented Alderson's intrusion at a critical moment when the Whittingham girl was being taken over."

"Taken over?"

"Don't stare at me like that. How do I know precisely what occurred? All I do know is that something must have happened, something did happen to produce the result I discovered."

Jameson looked baffled.

"Three men," continued Harper, giving it emphasis. "In green suits, matching green ties, grey shirts and collars. Three men wearing uniforms with which nobody is familiar. Why haven't those uniforms been recognized?"

"Because they were not uniforms at all," Jameson hazarded. "They merely looked that way, having a sort of official cut, let us say."

"Or because they were uniforms that nobody knows about," suggested Harper. "Because the government has said nothing to anybody. Because officialdom hasn't breathed a word to a soul. Is the taxpayer always told where his money is going?"

"What the devil are you getting at?"

"We're pulling the Moon to pieces and nobody thinks anything of it. It's been going on long enough to have become commonplace. A moon-boat is now about as remarkable as a Cunarder used to be. We're so sophisticated about such matters that we've lost the capacity for surprise."

"I'm aware of all this, since I live in the present," said Jameson, a trifle impatiently. "What of it?"

"Who's cooked up notions of exploiting Venus or Mars? Have you sent anyone there to take a look and, if so, when was it? Are they due back by now? Were they three men in green uniforms with grey shirts?"

"My God!" ejaculated Jameson, becoming visibly strained.

"Three men went somewhere, got more than they bargained for, involuntarily brought it back to spread around. That's my theory. Try it for size."

"If I approach the proper quarter with such a fantasy they'll think I'm cracked."

"I know why you fear that; I can read your mind, remember? Firstly, you personally know of no space-expedition, have heard not the slightest hint of one. Secondly, you cannot credit my diagnosis. Right?"

"Fat lot of use denying it."

"Then look at it this way: I know even if you don't that for a fragmentary moment I touched a genuinely alien mind in possession of a human body. That entity could not have solidified out of sheer nothingness. It must have arrived in some concealed manner. Somebody must have brought it. The only possible suspects are those three men."

"Go on," encouraged Jameson.

"We have not the vaguest notion how long those three have been gallivanting around. Maybe for a week, maybe for a year." He fixed his listener with an accusative stare. "Therefore the Whittingham girl may not be the first or by any means the last. That trio may have given the treatment to a hundred and be busily tending to a hundred more while we're sitting here making useless noises. If we continue to flatten our fannies long enough they'll enslave half the world before we wake up."

Jameson fidgeted and gloomed hesitantly at the phone.

"Brockman of Special Services," said Harper. "He's the guy you've got in mind right now." He made an urgent gesture. "All right, get through to him. What is there to lose? Perhaps he'll tell you what he wouldn't dream of telling me. Ask him if an expedition is out in space and when it's due back."

"Ten to one he'll ignore the question and want to know why I'm asking," Jameson protested. "I can hardly offer him your notions, and second hand at that."

"He'll try to pull down your pants only if there's no such

expedition," Harper asserted. "But if in fact there is one, and it's a top secret, your query will make his moustache drop off, if he has a moustache. He'll hotfoot over to find how the news got out. Try him and let's hear what he says."

Doubtfully, Jameson picked up the phone, said in resigned tones, "Get me Special Services Department, Mr. Brockman."

When the call went through Jameson spoke in the reluctant manner of one compelled to announce the arrest of Snow White and all the seven dwarfs.

"We're on to something peculiar here. I won't take up your time with the full details. It would help considerably if you can tell me whether a new space-venture has been made in secret." He listened a bit while his expression gradually went flat. "Yes, it's highly important that we should know one way or the other. Will you? Thanks a lot!" He planted the phone.

"He doesn't know?" said Harper.

"Correct."

"Should he know?"

"I assumed that he would. I could be wrong. The more highly confidential a piece of knowledge, the fewer entrusted with it and the further we'll have to seek for an answer, if there is a satisfactory answer." Taking a large blue handkerchief from his breast pocket he mopped his brow although he was not perspiring. "Brockman will call back as soon as he can make it."

"It would save valuable time to ring the White House and ask the President. Don't tell me *he* won't know what's going on."

Jameson was shocked. "Look, leave me to handle this in my own way, will you?"

"Sure. But the longer we take over this the sooner you may start handling things in some unearthly way." Harper registered a sour grin. "Not having my gun I'd then be forced to strangle you with my own hands—if I could do so without *you* taking *me* over."

"Shut up!" ordered Jameson, looking slightly sick. He scowled at the phone which promptly emitted a yelp. The unexpectedness of it made him jerk in his chair. He snatched it up, said, "Well?" let half a dozen expressions run over his face. Then he racked the phone, came to his feet, said, "They want us over there immediately."

"And we know why, don't we?"

Offering no response, Jameson led the way down, got into a car driven by an agent who resembled a cross between a haberdashery salesman and a wrestling champ. They rolled ten blocks, went up to the twentieth floor of a glass and concrete building, entered an office in which waited four serious men.

These four glanced briefly at Harper without recognizing him despite all the recent publicity. Apparently they rarely got around to reading the newspapers or watching the video.

The oldest of the quartet, a lean-faced individual with sharp eyes and fine white hair, snapped at Jameson, "What's all this about a space-expedition? Where did you pick up such a story?"

Seeing nothing for it but to pass the buck, Jameson indicated his companion. "This is Wade Harper. State police have him tagged as a murderer. He came to us an hour or so ago. My query arose from his story."

Four pairs of eyes shifted to Harper. "What story?"

These men were edgy and Harper could see it. He could also see why they had the willies: they were deeply concerned about reserved data becoming public property. And he could see, too, that for the moment Jameson had forgotten his special aptitude. It isn't easy for people to become accustomed to an almost mythical abnormality in the thoroughly normal-looking.

Addressing the white-haired man, he filched his name and said, "Mr. King, I know for a fact that eighteen months ago we sent a ship to Venus, the nearest planet. That ship was the result of twenty years of governmental experimentation. It bore a crew of three hand-picked men. Its return has two alternative dates. If the crew found conditions unbearable the ship should have been back last November. If conditions permit them to exist and indulge a little exploration they're due in mid June, about five weeks hence. The fact that they are not known to have returned is officially considered encouraging. The government awaits their arrival before giving the news to the world."

King heard all this with facial impassivity that he fondly imagined concealed his boiling thoughts. He asked with forced calmness, "And how did you obtain this information?"

It was too much for Jameson who had listened with amazement to the recital and been awakened by it. "This man is telepathic Mr. King. He has proved it to my satisfaction. He has picked the facts out of your mind."

"Indeed?" King was openly sceptical. "Then how do you account for the nature of your call to Brockman twenty minutes ago?"

"I suspected it then," Harper chipped in. "But now I *know*." He studied King levelly, added, "At the moment you're thinking that if the world is to be afflicted with such creatures as telepaths it might be a good thing to put them out of harm's way, and fast."

"You know too much," said King. "No government could function with any degree of security with people like you hanging around."

"I've been hanging around enough years to make me wish they were fewer. We haven't had a bloody revolution yet."

"But we have a suspected murderer dragged into a government office by a departmental director of the F.B.I.," said King, making it sound like a legitimate grievance. "It is certainly a new and previously unheard-of-practice. I hope they had the forethought to search you for concealed weapons."

By Harper's side Jameson reddened and interjected, "Pardon me, Mr. King, but there is far more to this issue than the aspect that seems to irritate you."

"Such as what?"

"The ship is back," Harper put in.

All four jerked as though stabbed with needles.

King demanded, "When did it return? Where did it land?"

"I don't know."

They relaxed, suddenly confident that Harper was talking through the rear of his neck.

"Then how do you know it is back?"

"He found a trace of the crew," informed Jameson. "Or that's how it looks."

Harper contradicted carefully, "No, I don't think I did. I think the crew is dead."

"So the crew died and you've not the faintest notion of where their ship is planted?" inquired King, by this time toying with the theory that Harper was off his nut but puzzled to find a plausible reason why so shrewd an individual as Jameson had become equally cracked. "Nevertheless you *know* that the ship has returned?"

"I'd bet a million dollars on it."

"It made the trip all on its ownsome? A unique spatial convulsion flung it thirty million miles or more across the void and dumped it someplace unknown to all and unsuspected by anyone but you?"

"Your sarcasm is pointless, doesn't help any and furthermore it gives me a pain in the seat," snapped Harper, becoming tough. "The ship was brought here by a bunch of Venusians. How d'you like that, eh?"

King didn't like it at all. His mind unhesitatingly rejected the bald statement, started sorting out a dozen objections and deciding which to voice first.

The bespectacled man on his right took advantage of the

pause to chip in and speak to Harper as one would do a wayward child.

"Piloting a space-ship is not an easy matter."

"No, Mr. Smedley, I guess it isn't."

"It's highly technical. It requires a great deal of know-how."

"That," said Harper, "is precisely the hell of it."

"What do you mean?"

"Anyone who can hijack a ship and run it forthwith, without any tuition, can take over anything else we've got with as little trouble." He gave them a few seconds to stew the point, then added for good measure, "Bit by bit, piece by piece, until they have everything and we have nothing— not even our souls."

"That idea is detestable," said King, beginning to feel cold.

"It should be," agreed Harper. "And further, you'd do well to abandon this latest notion you're concocting."

"What notion?"

"That I'm the agent of a scheming gang across the ocean who, in some mysterious way, are trying to pull a fast one. All that feuding is over as from today. They're in the same mess along with the rest of humanity and the sooner that's realized the better. They're going to become just as scared as I am right now."

"I doubt it. They'll be equally suspicious. They'll blame us for trying to disturb the world with a better and bigger bogey."

"It won't matter a cuss who blames who when we're no longer human. Come to that, we won't be mentally capable of apportioning blame."

King argued stubbornly, "It seems to me that you're taking a devil of a lot for granted on the basis of very little evidence. That evidence may be real enough to you. To us it comes secondhand. Even if we accept Jameson's statement that you are a genuine telepath, even if we take at face value the symptoms of it which you have displayed in this room, the fact remains that you're just as capable as anyone else of imagining things. I can conceive no logical reason for supposing that a telepath is impervious to delusions. Do you seriously expect us to alert the entire defences of this country on the strength of an unproven story?"

"No, I don't," admitted Harper. "I'm not that daft."

"Then what do you expect of us?"

"Firstly, I wanted official confirmation of my suspicion that a ship really has been sent somewhere beyond the Moon. That is why I came all the way here and avoided being picked up by local police who know too little and bark too much. Somehow or other I *had* to learn about that ship."

"Secondly?"

"I now expect action within reasonable limits. If it produces the proof you require I expect further action on a national scale."

"It is far easier to talk about getting proof than to go out and dig it up. If proof exists why didn't you find it yourself and bring it with you? Surely your own commonsense should tell you that the wilder a story the more proof it requires to make convincing?"

"I know," said Harper. "And I reckon I could have got enough to make you leap out of your shirt if only I'd possessed an item hidden in your top-secret files."

"To what are you referring?"

"The photographs of those three spacemen." He eyed King and his confrères with the sorrowful reproof of one surprised by their inability to perceive the obvious. "We have a witness who got a good, close look at two of those three and made careful note of them. Show him your pictures. If he says they're the boys, that settles it. The balloon goes up next minute."

Jameson waggled his eyebrows and put in, "Yes, that is the logical move. It should decide the matter one way or the other. We can do better than that, too. We can remove any element of doubt."

"How?" inquired King.

"That Thunderbug must have come from somewhere. It may have travelled hundreds of miles before reaching the fateful spot. A dozen, twenty or forty people may have noticed it and the three men with it. I can put agents on the job of tracing that back-track and finding the witnesses. If all of them say the same thing, namely, that those three men are your missing pilots——" He let it die out, thereby making it sound highly sinister.

"To enable you to do that," King pointed out, "we would have to get those photographs released from secret files and provide you with a large number of copies."

"Of course."

"But that means the general dissemination of reserved data."

Harper emitted a loud groan, rubbed his jaw and recited the names of the twelve apostles.

Staring at him distastefully, King said, "I'll see what the appropriate department decides."

"While you're at it," Harper suggested, "you can persuade some other appropriate department to seize the body of Jocelyn Whittingham and subject it to an expert autopsy. I don't know whether that will tell us anything, but it might. The bet is worth taking, anyway."

"I'll see what they decide," repeated King. He went out with visible unwillingness. The remaining three fidgeted and registered the discomfort of men compelled to hold a buck that cannot be passed.

"Have you got a gun?" Harper asked Jameson.

"Yes."

"Better hold on to it good and tight."

"Why?"

"Because if he gets nowhere with the higher-ups I'm going to run amok."

"You'd better not!" warned Jameson.

"I'd rather die quickly in a fracas here than slowly some-place else," said Harper fervently.

The three watched him with open apprehension.

King was gone a long time. Eventually he returned with a heavily built, military-looking man named Benfield. The latter grasped three large photographs which he exhibited to Harper as he spoke.

"Know these fellows?"

"No."

"Sure of that?"

"I'm positive. They're complete strangers to me."

"Humph! Can you say that they answer to the descriptions of the trio you have in mind?"

"Fairly well. I could be more definite if those pics were in colour. The uniforms convey nothing in black and white."

"They are dark green uniforms with silver buttons, grey shirts, green ties."

"Apart from the silver buttons the details match up."

"All right. We'll make an immediate check. Who's this witness?"

Harper told him about the oldster at the filling station while Benfield made note of it on a scratch-pad.

Benfield said to Jameson, "We'll try this one first. If the check proves confirmatory we'll run off enough clear copies to enable your men to follow the back trail. Meanwhile, we'll radio a set to your office out there. Won't take them long to determine whether or not this is a gag, will it?"

"A couple of hours," said Jameson.

"A couple of minutes would be better," observed Harper. "And how about taking the heat off me while you're at it?"

"We'll think about that when the report comes in. If it makes hay of your story we'd better have you examined by a mental specialist."

"That would be fun," Harper assured. "He'd play all the

kings and I'd play all the aces. In the end you'd have to put *him* away."

Benfield let it pass. He was taking this tale of telepathic power and all the rest of the story with a sizeable dose of salt. The sole feature that impressed him was that somehow or other a wanted felon had succeeded in talking his way into the higher echelons of Washington. That suggested either a modicum of incredible truth or a superb gift of the gab. But he was just. He was willing to pursue the matter for the sake of finding any factual grain that might be lying around.

"Put him somewhere safe," Benfield ordered Jameson, "and hold him until we get our reply."

Harper protested, "D'you think I'm going to run off after coming all the way here?"

"No, I don't think so—because you're not going to be given the chance." He threw Jameson a look of warning, departed with the photographs in his hand.

"We'll phone you at your H.Q. immediately we hear," promised King. He stared Harper out of face in effort to reassert authority, continued to stare at the other's broad back as he went out. But his thoughts skittered wildly around and were not free from fear.

Sitting boredly in Jameson's office Harper said, "Thanks for the lunch. Before long you can buy me dinner as well." He glanced at his wrist-watch. "It's three-forty. Why don't they report direct to you? They're your men, aren't they?"

"They have their orders."

"Yes, I know. Orders from somebody else. At this moment you're pondering the fact that this business isn't properly within your bailiwick. The F.B.I. has been called upon to hunt most everything but prodigal space-pilots. That's how you look at it. And you can't decide whether anything is likely to come of it."

"We'll know in due course."

"They're taking long enough to find out." Harper brooded silently for a couple of minutes, then showed alarm. "What if that oldster is dead and no longer able to identify anything?"

"Any particular reason why he might be?" inquired Jameson, surveying him keenly.

"Yes. Those three may have figured things out for themselves and returned to shut his mouth."

"Why should they do that? Miss Whittingham's evidence cleared them of suspicion. To involve themselves afresh would be a singularly stupid move; it would redirect attention their way after they've succeeded in averting it."

"You're examining it from the wrong angle," declared Harper, "and you err on two counts."

"Name them."

"For one, you're assuming that if guilty they will behave like any other Earthborn thugs who've killed a cop. But why should they? The crime doesn't mean the same to them. For all I know to the contrary they thought as little of it as does some thick-headed farmer who sees a strange bird in the woods, points his gun and shoots it. Maybe it was the rarest bird in the world, now made extinct. Does he give a damn?"

"That's pretty good reason why they should not come back to shut up the witness," Jameson pointed out. "They don't care enough to bother."

"It's nothing of the sort. It's an argument against your supposition that Alderson's death should be their primary concern. I reckon they've a worry far bigger."

"Such as what?"

"Fear of being identified too soon. They're not anxious to be recognized as spacemen and never mind the criminal angle. To be spotted as the missing space-crew would start up a transcontinental hunt. At this stage they don't want to be recognized and pursued. They need time to do whatever they've come here to do."

75

"Since you're so well-informed," commented Jameson, a trifle sardonically, "perhaps you can reveal their purpose in coming."

"God alone knows. But it's a dirty one. Why else should they try do it on the sly? An honest motive warrants an open approach. The skulker in the shadows is up to no good."

"You may be making the very same mistake that you've just tied on to me," said Jameson. "You're weighing them up in human terms. That's not a good way of judging alien purposes, is it?"

Harper sniffed his contempt. "In so far as their actions affect us we must look at them from our own viewpoint. It may well be that they are justifiably rated as the greatest adventurers and biggest patriots in Venusian history. But if their loyal shenanigans are going to cost me a toenail they're a trio of prize stinkers so far as I'm concerned."

"I agree with you there."

"All right. Now that old geezer at the filling station cannot possibly finger them for the murder of Alderson. The most he can do with respect to that is point suspiciously. His evidence wouldn't hang them in a month of Sundays." He leaned forward, gaze intent. "But what he *can* do is exactly what they're trying to get him to do right now. He can look at three pictures, give the nod and start the hunt. There's only one sure way to prevent him and that is by closing his trap for keeps before it's too late."

"That's clear enough reasoning," said Jameson, "but it has one major flaw."

"What is it?"

"All the news channels have publicized details of both the Alderson and Whittingham killings. Everyone from coast to coast knows that you're wanted for the latter and suspected of the former. The three fugitives know that they don't fit in this picture and that, in any event, your witness's description of them would fit a thousand others. There's nothing whatever in the news to suggest the remotest likelihood of a witness being shown photographs dug out of confidential files in Washington. So why should they deduce that possibility?"

"Because I shot down the Whittingham girl."

"I don't understand," confessed Jameson, frowning.

"Look, I've given you the facts as I saw them. They picked up that girl for some reason or other, probably because the opportunity presented itself and they wanted to try their technique. Maybe they're missionaries making converts and pass up no chances on the general principle of the more the merrier. Anyway, they turned her into another of their own kind. She ceased to be Jocelyn Whittingham but continued to masquerade as such. Don't ask me how it was done because I don't know and can't guess."

"Well?"

"The big question now is: were they able to learn and remember that girl's Earth-identity? Or was it something they failed to record either because they viewed it as of no consequence or because it was incomprehensible to them?"

"Go on," Jameson encouraged.

"If they don't know her identity the news of her death will mean nothing to them. It will look just like any other sordid murder and they won't realize they're linked with it in any way. But if they *do* know her identity——"

"For crime's sake, don't keep me in suspense," pleaded Jameson.

"The killing will get them on to their roller-skates and going at top speed. They'll want to know why she was killed. They'll want to know whether she died because a Venusian can be recognized and, if so, how and by whom. They can see with half an eye that real knowledge of their presence will inevitably be linked with that space-expedition and they'll be eager to find out whether there's time to break the linkage by cutting a couple of throats."

"Including yours."

"Yes. I'm the sacrificial goat. The news-channels have

shouted my name and address all over the shop and invited them to come and get me—if they can. It won't be a quick death, either. They'll do me in slowly, very slowly."

"What makes you say that?"

"So far as I can guess they've one weapon and one only. But it's a formidable one. They can double as human beings without possibility of detection except by some freak like myself. It's of the greatest importance to them to find out how I did it. Without that knowledge they can't take steps to prevent it happening again. They can't counter a menace without knowing the nature of it. They will have to get the truth out of me in any way it can be done, no matter how bloody and no matter at what risk. Otherwise there's no telling how many more folk can tag them or when the next moment will be their last. Their lives wouldn't be worth living."

"Telepaths aren't ten a penny," Jameson pointed out. "You've said so yourself."

"But *they* don't know that. They're left guessing in circumstances where no guess is too far-fetched. To them, it might well be that every red-haired human can smell them— and there are a deuce of a lot of redheads around. They've *got* to know how it's done."

"You're no carrot-top," said Jameson, "but if someday we find you lying around without your scalp we'll consider it fair evidence of your veracity."

"Thanks," conceded Harper. "You boys have a good time over my body. Enjoy a few hearty laughs while there remains something to snicker about. Won't be long before you'll wish you were me!"

"You know I was only ribbing. I——"

He grabbed the phone before it had time to give a proper whirr, held it to his ear. Harper came to his feet, looking anticipatory.

"Same as before," Jameson told him, replacing the instrument and reaching for his hat. "They want us over at once. We might as well have stayed there in the first place."

"Something has broken," declared Harper as they hustled outside and clambered into the car. "If those pics had proved to be duds they'd have said so, with acid for sauce. They wouldn't drag us ten blocks merely to tell us the check proved a flop. Or would they? After all, it's the taxpayers' gas we're using."

Jameson sat tight-faced and offered no comment.

Chapter 6

There were only two men waiting this time. One had stern, leathery features famous throughout the world: General Conway, tall, grey-haired, distinguished. The other one was Benfield, now decidedly grim.

"So!" rumbled General Conway, fixing Harper with a cold eye. "You are the mind-reader?"

"Putting it that way makes me seem like a vaudeville act," said Harper, far from overawed.

"Quite probably," agreed the general, thinking it wasn't so far removed either. He examined the other carefully from the shoes up, letting his gaze linger longest on a pair of thick and exceedingly hairy wrists. His mental diagnosis was not flattering: it determined the subject to be a powerful and presumably intelligent man who would have the misfortune to look like an ape when in officer's uniform. Too broad, squat and hirsute to fit the part of a captain or colonel.

Harper said informatively, "That's nothing. You ought to

see me naked. I resemble a curly rug. Hence the word rugged."

The general stiffened authoritatively. Jameson looked appalled. Benfield was too preoccupied to have any reaction.

"If you know what is in my mind there's little need to speak," declared General Conway, annoyed at the loss of his privacy. "What does it tell you?"

"An awful ruckus has started," replied Harper without hesitation. "And I'm certified sane."

The other nodded. "Your witness has confirmed that the men in that car were the same three who set out for Venus about eighteen months ago. The F.B.I. is following their trail forward and backward and already has found two more witnesses who say the same." He rested on a table-edge, folded his arms, gazed steadily at his listener. "This is a most serious business."

"It'll get worse," Harper promised. "If that is any consolation."

"This is a poor time for levity," reproved the general. "We are treating the matter with the importance it deserves. All forces of law and order in the west are combining in effort to trace that Thunderbug back to its starting-point in the hope that the ship may be located in that area. A forward trace is also being made despite that it's likely to prove futile, the machine having been abandoned by this time."

"Neither the ship nor the car matter very much. It's those three rampaging——"

"We are after those as well," Conway interrupted. "All police, military and ancillary organizations have been or soon will be alerted. Photographs, fingerprint formulae and other necessary information is being distributed as fast as we can produce. The capture is being given top priority, all other criminological investigations to be dropped pending its achievement. Unfortunately, at this stage we cannot warn the public as a whole without creating widespread alarm and consequences that may get out of control."

"Good enough," approved Harper. "So this is where I go out."

"On the contrary, this is where you stay in. We have got you and intend to keep you. There's a war on and you're drafted."

"Then I apply for indeterminate leave forthwith."

"Permission denied," snapped Conway, too concerned even to smile. He walked around the table, sat behind it, let his fingers tap restlessly on its surface. "The air forces are out in full strength scouting for that ship. Every civilian plane that can be mustered is under orders to assist. We have confiscated the bodies of that girl and the trooper, handed them over to scientists for special examination. Everything that can be done has been or soon will be done. The issue of the moment is that of how to deal with you."

"Me?"

"Yes. There are a lot of questions that must be answered. Firstly, have you any explanation of your telepathic power? Can you say how it originated?"

"No."

"It just happened?"

"So far as I can recall I was born that way."

"H'm!" Conway was dissatisfied, went on. "We are making exhaustive search into the backgrounds of your parents and grandparents. If possible, we must discover the reason why you are what you are."

"Personally," remarked Harper, "I couldn't care less about the reason. It has never interested me."

"It interests us. We must determine as soon as we can whether any more of your kind may be hanging around and, if so, in what number. Also whether there is any positive method of finding them and conscripting them until this crisis is over."

"After which they in turn will be treated from the crisis

viewpoint," thrust Harper. "And your big problem will be how to put them out of harm's way until such time as they may be needed again."

"Now see here——"

"I know what you're thinking and you cannot conceal it from me. I know that authority is squatting on the horns of a large and sharp-pointed dilemma. A telepath is a menace to those in power but a protection against foes such as we are facing right now. You cannot destroy the menace without hereby depriving yourselves of the protection. You cannot ensure mental privacy except at the prospective price of mental slavery. You're in a first-class jam that doesn't really exist because it's purely imaginary and born of the conditioning of non-telepathic minds."

Conway made no attempt to dispute this vigorous revealing of his thoughts. He sat in silence, his cold attention on Harper, spoke only when he had finished.

"And what makes you say that there is no such quandary?"

"Because all the irrational bigots swarming on this cockeyed world invariably jump to the conclusion that anyone radically different from themselves must be bad. It inflates badly shrivelled egos to look at things that way. Every man his own paragon of virtue and goodness." He glowered at General Conway and said with ire, "A telepath has a code of ethics fully as good as anyone else's and perhaps a damnsight better because he has to beat off more temptation. I don't listen unless circumstances make it necessary. I don't hear unless I'm shouted at."

The other was blunt enough to appreciate straight talk. He was openly impressed. Leaning back in his chair he surveyed Harper afresh.

"We've done a deal of checking on you already. You heard Trooper Alderson from a distance of approximately six hundred yards. Without listening, I presume?"

"I heard his death-cry. On the neural hand it's as effective as a scream. I couldn't help hearing."

"You have helped nail a number of wanted criminals and it is now obvious how you did it. But you never listen?"

"Guilt yells across the street. Fear bellows like an angry bull."

"Is there *anything* that broadcasts on a level sufficiently muted to escape your attention?"

"Yes—ordinary, everyday, innocent thoughts."

"You do not listen to those?"

"Why on earth should I bother? Do you try to sort out every spoken word from the continual hum of conversation around you in a restaurant? Does a busy telephone operator take time off to absorb the babble going through her switchboard? If I went around trying to pick up everything that's going I'd have qualified for a strait jacket ten years ago. Continual, ceaseless yap can torture a telepath unless he closes his mind to it."

By now Conway was three-quarters convinced. His mind had made considerable readjustment. He resumed his table-tapping, cast an inquiring glance at Benfield and Jameson. They immediately put on the blank expressions of impartial onlookers not qualified to make decisions.

"I understand," continued Conway, "that to date you have not encountered another telepath?"

"No," agreed Harper regretfully.

"But if two of you passed by without listening, neither of you would become aware of the other's existence?"

"I suppose so. But I couldn't swear to it. If we radiate more powerfully than the average human——"

"Yes, but your lack of contact is no proof of your uniqueness? For all we know to the contrary there may be fifty or a hundred telepaths in this very city?"

"I think it most unlikely but wouldn't define it as impossible."

"What is your effective range?" asked Conway.

"About eight hundred yards. It varies from time to time. On rare occasions I have received at three times that distance. Other times it drops to a hundred or less."

"Do you know the cause of such variation? Is it due to the nature of surroundings, blanking by big buildings or anything similar?"

"I could not say for sure, not having subjected the matter to systematic test. Surroundings make no difference and that's all I'm certain about."

"But you have a theory?" Conway pressed.

"Yes," admitted Harper. "I suspect that on any given occasion my range is determined by the amplitude of the other person's radiations. The more powerfully he broadcasts the greater the distance over which I can pick him up. The weaker, the less a distance. As I've said, it would require scientific tests to establish the truth or falsity of that notion."

"Are you willing to undergo such tests?"

"I am not," declared Harper, showing pugnacity.

"Why not?"

"The immediate problem is not that of what to do about telepaths. It's that of what to do about invading Venusians. Nobody is going to use me for a guinea-pig. Go pick on the quarry you're already hunting. They've done plenty and aim to do a lot more. My only crime is that of performing a public service."

"Don't view it in that light, Mr. Harper," Conway soothed. "We appreciate to the full the excellent part you have played. The trouble is that we're not satisfied. We want more of you. We want all you can give. In fact we need it so badly that we demand it as of right."

"What do you require of me?"

"All the information we can get out of you now and perhaps some action later."

"Go ahead. Let no man say Wade Harper was unable to suffer."

Conway signed to Benfield. "Switch on that tape-recorder." He returned his attention to Harper. "This one is of the utmost importance. I want you to answer it with the greatest clarity you can command. What impelled you to shoot Jocelyn Whittingham?"

"That's a tough question," Harper replied. "I cannot translate it in terms you can understand; it's like trying to describe a rose to a man blind from birth."

"Never mind. Do your best."

"All right. It was somewhat like this: you're in your wife's bedroom. You notice a new and pretty jewel-box on her dressing-table. Full of curiosity, you open it. The thing contains a live whip-snake. The snake sees you the same instant. It leaps out. Despite the shock you act fast. You swipe it in mid air, knock it to the floor, crush it under heel. That's how it was."

"I see." Conway stared at him thoughtfully, then asked, "Can't you express it in manner more in keeping with what actually happened?"

"She started up the steps. I knew she might be the girl I was seeking. I made a stab at her mind for the sole purpose of identifying her. The moment I touched I realized what I had touched. At the same moment——"

"*What* did you touch?" inquired Conway.

"Something not human. I cannot describe it more accurately. I planted a telepathic hand fairly and squarely on the slimy mental field of a non-human entity. At the same instant it felt my touch. That was additional confirmation if any were needed, because no normal human being can sense a telepathic probe. I realized several things in that split-second. Firstly, she didn't know whence the probe had come. She had no directional sense such as I possess. But she correctly assumed that it came from me because I was in plain sight and already racing toward her."

"She did not *know* it was you?" repeated Conway. "You

mean she was in no way telepathic herself?"

"I hadn't any evidence of it. There was only that abnormal sensitivity which, I suppose, has been developed as a defence-mechanism some place else. She did know beyond all doubt that suddenly and without warning a strange and dangerous mind had lifted her mask and seen beneath. She gave out a panicky thought that she must get away, she must warn the others that they're not as well-hidden as they think, that they *can* be exposed."

"A—a—ah!" Conway displayed hopefulness. "So she knew the precise location of these others? She knew how to get into touch with them?"

"If so," said Harper, "her mind did not admit it. Things were moving fast. We were both thunderstruck by the encounter. Her mind was yelling, '*Escape, escape, escape!*' while mine ordered imperatively, '*Stop her, stop, stop . . . kill, kill!*' I shot her down without any compunctions whatsoever. I'd quite forgotten that she was a girl or had been a girl. For the moment she was something else, something that had to be laid good and cold. I gave her the magazine right through the bean. I heard the alien mentality cease sizzling and fade to nothingness. That showed it could die just the same as anybody else."

"Then you went away without making further examination?"

"I did. I went fast. I'd no time for further horsing around. I didn't dare risk being picked up anywhere but here. To tell this story in any police barracks or sheriff's office, where they didn't know the score, would eventually land me in an asylum."

"Couldn't you have saved time, trouble and anxiety by calling us long distance?"

"How far would I have got that way? Some underling would have listened, smirked knowingly and sent police to the booth to pick up a loony. I've had a tough enough job reaching the right people in person. At that I reckon

I'm lucky. I hope to make it to the Pearly Gates with less trouble."

None of the listeners relished that remark but were unable to deny the truth of it. A formidable guard of minor officials stood between the high executive and a besieging force of malcontents, theorists, halfwits and world-doomers. Perforce they also held at bay the rare individual with something genuinely worth hearing.

General Conway harumphed, decided that there were no satisfactory methods of overcoming this difficulty, went on to say, "You have made contact with an alien life-form. So far as we know you're the only one who has done so and remained able and willing to talk about it. Can you add anything that may help us to determine the true nature of the foe?"

"I didn't see it with my own two eyes. Therefore I cannot assist you with an accurate description."

"Quite so. But you must have gained some kind of an impression."

Thinking it over, Harper conceded, "Yes, that's true."

"Let us have it. No matter how vague or fleeting, we need every datum we can get on this subject."

"For no apparent reason I felt that alien ownership of another body is a natural phenomenon. That is to say, I knew more or less instinctively that the thing occupying the body of Jocelyn Whittingham was functionally designed for such a purpose, was perfectly at home and knew how to use what it had gained. The girl was a human being from toes to hair in all respects but one: another and different life-spark had been substituted."

"Which suggests that its nature is wholly parasitic?" asked Conway. "It normally exists in possession of some other life-form?"

"Yes. It's an old hand at that game."

"And that in turn suggests that when it acquires another

body it also gains the data within the brain, all the knowledge, the memory and so forth?"

"Undoubtedly. It could not survive without doing so. Otherwise its own incompetence would betray it at once."

Turning his attention to Benfield, the general remarked, "The inevitable deduction is that Venus harbours various life-forms, some of which are the natural prey of a possessive parasite. Also that this parasite is capable of taking over a form higher than any in its own habitat. It can adapt right out of its own environment and, if I may put it that way, it can raise itself by its own bootstraps."

Benfield nodded agreement.

"Also," continued Conway, "it is probably microscopic or germlike. That's my guess. I'll have to leave that angle to others more expert. They'll be able to make shrewder estimates of its characteristics."

"It would help more than somewhat if we could discover how that girl was mastered," Harper pointed out. "Her body might tell the story."

"That is being looked into. We have confiscated her corpse despite violent objections from her relatives."

Harper looked at him, eyes glowing. "Which of them raised the biggest outcry?"

About to add something more, Conway paused, closed his mouth, opened it, registered momentary bafflement.

"Why?"

"We Venusians must stick together."

"You mean——?"

"Yes, I mean what you're now thinking."

Firming his lips, Conway reached for the phone, ordered, "Take the entire Whittingham family into safe keeping at once. No, it is not an arrest. There are no charges. Tell them it's for their own protection. Eh? If their lawyer chips in, refer him directly to me."

"That will do a fat lot of good," remarked Harper. "If one or more of the Whittinghams is no longer of this world you're helping him create a bunch of Venusian cops out west."

"It's a risk we'll have to take."

"Not necessarily. You could put them in animal cages and feed them with long tongs. Anything, anything so long as they can't get near enough to help themselves to their own guards."

"That would be gross violation of their constitutional rights. We could get away with such tactics only by justifying them before the public. To do that we must release information that we wish to preserve, at least for the time being." His eyes questioned Harper as if to say, "What's the answer to that?"

Harper took it up promptly. "Tell them the truth. Tell the Whittinghams that Jocelyn died of a new, malignant and highly contagious disease. They must be isolated until found free from it. The black plague again."

"What, when they know she was shot?"

"*I* had the disease. I was raving mad with it. I touched her, contaminated her. She's lucky to be dead. You've got to give a clean bill of health to whoever handled her afterward. Scare them with a yarn like that. Some clause in the health laws can be finagled to cover their incarceration. No protectors of civil liberties are going to bawl about the freedom of suspected lepers. And the story will be substantially true, won't it?"

"You may have something there." Conway used the phone again, gave instructions, finished, "Consult Professor Holzberger about the technical description of a suitable pretext. What is needed is something strong enough to convince but not strong enough to cause a panic." He ended, said to Harper, "And now what?"

"When there's a chance, let me go out there to look them over. If I find them all clean, give them a mock check-up by some worried-looking medico, then let them go. They'll be too relieved to gripe."

"But if one of them is possessed?"

"I'll smell him at first sniff. He'll know it, too. Keep him at all costs. When the others have gone, pull him apart and see if you can find the pea in his whistle. You could do that without a qualm. So far as humanity is concerned he's already dead. You'll be carving an animated corpse. With luck you might be able to isolate whatever is combing his hair."

Conway frowned. Jameson looked slightly sick. Benfield didn't enjoy it either; he was visualizing his hands shaving himself at another's behest.

"We'll take that up shortly," said Conway. "There is one more cogent point yet to be considered. You say that the instant you recognized the Whittingham girl her immediate thought was of escape?"

"Yes."

"But not to a specific place?"

"No."

"Therefore her impulse to flee was instinctive and no more?"

"Not entirely. She experienced the shock of somebody deprived without warning of a long-established and greatly valued truth, namely, that recognition is impossible. She was confronted with an irrefutable datum contrary to all experience. She felt the dire need to get away from me and tell the others."

"Which others? *Where*?"

"I don't know."

"You know only that *she* didn't know?"

Harper fidgeted around, brooded at the floor. "Frankly, I'm unable to give a satisfactory answer. Possibly she didn't have the remotest notion of where the others might be and in that respect had been made irrational by the crisis. Or she may have known but succeeded in suppressing the knowledge, which I doubt. Or——"

"Or what?"

"She may have possessed some alien sense which enables her kind to contact each other. A sense we haven't got and cannot understand. Something like the homing instinct of pigeons or dogs, but on a species basis."

"But you are convinced that she was not telepathic?"

"Not in the way that I am."

"In some other way, perhaps?"

"Nothing is impossible," said Harper flatly. "It is beyond my power to list the attributes of things native to some place umpteen millions of miles away after a one-second glance. Catch me another dozen. I'll take a longer look and tell you more."

Responding to Conway's gesture, Benfield switched off the tape-recorder.

"Catch you another dozen," echoed Conway. "How the devil are we going to do that? We know of three, and it's not beyond our resources to find and seize them sooner or later. Getting any others who may be around is a different matter. We have nothing to go upon, no details concerning them, no way of identifying them." His gaze came up, levelled on Harper. "Excepting through you. That's why you're drafted. We require your services to test every suspect we can lay hands on."

"So I'm expected to stay put, wait for your lineups, look them over and say yes or no?"

"Exactly. There is no other way."

"There is," Harper contradicted.

"For instance?"

"You could use me for bait."

"Eh?"

"They want my matted corpus as badly as you want theirs. They need to learn what makes me a nuisance fully as much as you need to learn about them. In that respect they have an advantage. You must try to grab an unknown number of unknown pseudo-people. They have to snatch one man whose name, address and car tag number have been shouted all over the country. I'm the most desirable subject for vivisection they ever heard about since their last picnic on Saturn. Give them half a chance and they'll swarm around me drooling. All you need do is step in and pinch everyone holding a scalpel."

Conway breathed heavily and objected, "It's a risk, a grave risk."

"Think I'm tickled pink about it?"

"If anything should go wrong we'll have lost our most effective counter-weapon and be without means to replace it."

"The beauty of that will be," said Harper cheerfully, "that I will no longer care one-tenth of a damn. The dead are splendidly indifferent about who wins a war or gains a world."

"Perhaps not. But we'll still be living."

"That won't concern me either. My great-grandmother doesn't give a hoot about the hole in my sock."

"And *you* may still be living," retorted Conway. "Even though dead."

"I'll be a goner either way," Harper gave back with ghoulish philosophy. "What if some midget alien *is* wearing me like mink?"

He grinned at them, enjoying the repulsion in their minds.

The general was like a chess-player trying to decide whether mate could be ensured by sacrificing his queen. He was far from positive about it but could think up no satisfactory alternative. To his military mind, telepaths were expendable providing the supply of them was unending. Unfortunately they were neither shells nor guns. They could not be manufactured to order. So far as could be determined he had one and only one telepathic weapon in his armoury. If that one went there'd be no more.

Even if people with supernormal faculties existed in sufficient number to dispose of this extra-terrestrial menace once and for all, the situation would remain critical. There would come the aftermath. What of them? Could they be trusted to let the world go by? Or would experience of recent events waken them to their own power, tempt them to unite and confiscate the planet? They'd have a good excuse for doing so, an excuse convincing enough to sway the masses: only we could save you last time, only we can save you next time.

Conway was still stewing it over when again his phone called for attention. He took it meditatively, listened, abruptly came to full attention.

"Who? When did this happen? Yes, yes, you'd better." He cradled it, scowled forward.

"Something wrong?" asked Harper.

"You know what's wrong. You must have heard the details being recorded in my mind."

"I wasn't listening. I was full of my own thoughts. I can't make noises at myself and at the same time take note of other people's cerebral trumpetings."

"One of the witnesses is dead; the old man at the filling station."

"Murdered?"

"Yes. It happened a couple of hours ago but they found him only within the last fifteen minutes. Whoever did it has a good head start." Conway cocked an inquiring eye at Jameson. "I don't know what to think of it. You've far more experience in such matters. Do you suppose this may be mere coincidence?"

"How was he killed?" Jameson asked.

"They discovered him lying by his pumps, his skull crushed by a single blow from a heavy instrument. They say it looks as if he filled somebody's tank and was struck down when he tried to collect."

"Any evidence of robbery? Had his pockets been emptied or the cash register cleaned out?"

"No."

"H'm. That doesn't indicate that robbery wasn't the motive," Jameson opined. "The culprits may have been scared off before they could complete the job. Or maybe they were joyriders who slugged him for a free tank of alk, overdid it and made it murder." He pursed his lips while he mused a bit, finished, "These isolated filling stations get more than their fair share of rough stuff and have done for years. I think it's quite likely that this is a genuine coincidence. To treat it as of special significance may cause us to lose time chasing up the wrong alley."

Conway turned attention to Harper. "The police out there feel hamstrung because they're under strict orders to abandon everything in favour of the hunt for missing pilots. Yet one investigation may be part of the other and I don't want it to be temporarily ignored if there is a connection. On the other hand, I'd rather not countermand orders unless such a connection exists. What is your opinion?"

"If Venusians did it to shut the old fellow's trap, they arrived too late. He saw their photos and set the fireworks going before they could stop him. But *they* wouldn't know that."

"You think they did it and therefore this is not a coincidence?"

"No," said Harper carefully. "Jameson has given his viewpoint and I'm trying to consider its opposite. I'm telling you that if those three are aware of the identity of the girl they converted, her death will give them the shakes. Two and two make four on any planet. They'll add up the news, make it the correct total, decide she'd been found out somehow, God knows how."

"And so——?"

"They know a nation-wide hunt will be after them unless they can cover up. Even that will do no more than delay matters, but delay is all they need. If they can postpone capture long enough it will come too late. Many people spotted them in that Thunderbug but only two saw them actually with the girl, took a close look at them at the time. Those were Alderson and the oldster. The former is too dead to study pictures. It would help them some to have the latter in the same condition. That's how they'd look at it. The basic requirements of survival can be seen by any type of mind no matter where it's from."

"Then why were they so slow to get at him?" commented Conway. "They dealt with him three to four hours behind time."

"I killed that girl and came here as fast as I could go and have been hanging around all day. The news didn't break until some time after I'd left. If when they saw the news they had to rush back as far, or perhaps farther, they must have moved as swiftly as they dared. It takes time to cover territory even in these days."

"I suppose so." Doubtfully, Conway shifted gaze to Benfield. "Have you any ideas?"

"Yes, General. I think it best to pursue this matter in the principle of overlooking nothing."

"That's the boy," approved Harper. "With all the troops and police littering this country we should be able to spare a couple of dozen to chase a possibility. The grave loss of manpower won't make us topple any quicker."

Conway did not approve the humour, which smacked to him of unwarranted sarcasm. But it served its purpose of stinging him into immediate action. He handled the phone with the air of being fed up holding it, made his call.

"Williams, about that filling station murder. I want it looked into. Make it quick and thorough. Yes, orders are suspended with respect to this case only. It may be linked with the search. If so, one of the wanted men has been in that area today. Call me and report directly you make progress." He ended, gave a challenging look at the others. "That settles that. There's little more we can do until we make our first capture—and it's to be hoped we get him alive."

"It's also to be hoped that one will lead to the others," put in Benfield.

"And it's further to be hoped that some time before Christmas somebody will make up their mind about accepting or rejecting my offer to dangle on the hook," said Harper.

"Your first job is to check the Whittingham family," Conway shot back. "After that we'll consider what to do with you next."

"Then let's go." Harper waved a familiar good-bye to General Conway, performing it in the manner of a rookie too raw to know better. Conway involuntarily bristled at him, a fact he found most pleasing.

"There's no sense in going out of your way to irritate the old boy," reproved Jameson when they had exited and reached the car. "He has troubles enough."

"I was reasserting the freedom of the individual at the moment when it's likeliest to become disputed," snapped Harper. "And furthermore, a cat may look at a king. That holds good though the heavens fall."

Jameson did not choose to argue the point.

Back at headquarters Jameson said, "The sooner you get out there and do your stuff, the better. We'll send you by plane or copter. Sit down and wait—I'll find out what can be done."

"You can restore my good character while you're at it," Harper suggested. "Cancel that call for me. I don't like it even if it is being ignored. Priority of pilot-search won't prevent some sharp-eyed cuss grabbing me if he notices me right under his nose."

"We'll 'tend to that eventually. Meanwhile I'll send a couple of agents with you, to be on the safe side."

"Think I can't look after myself?"

"It's Conway's order."

"Oh, all right." As the other went through the door,

Harper called, "And I want my gun back. It's my property, isn't it?"

Jameson returned in two minutes, tossed him the weapon and a large brown envelope. "Study that while I get things moving—all planes are busy and you'll have to use a copter." He departed again.

Tucking the gun under his left arm, Harper extracted the envelope's flap, slid out three full-plate glossy photographs. Each had a typed slip of data attached to its back. He examined them closely.

The first was of William Gould, twenty-eight, test-pilot-in-chief, a frank-faced, blond-haired, husky individual who weighed one-eighty pounds and had a half-moon scar on the left brow. The thinner, dark-haired face smiling from the second picture was that of Cory McDonald, twenty-four, test-pilot and computer, a wiry type of one-fifty-five pounds, no identifying marks on body. Picture number three showed the thoughtful, serious features of Earl James Langley, twenty-seven, test-pilot and astronavigator, dark-haired, one-sixty-two pounds, small mole on right thigh, white scars on both kneecaps.

"Gould, McDonald and Langley," recited Harper to himself as he shuffled the photos to and fro and memorized the faces. "Gould, McDonald and Langley. Three good boys who went away full of hope and came back full of hell. God rest their souls!"

He felt vengeful as he looked at them. Didn't seem right that humanity's outward growth should be paid for by such as these. The salt of the earth thrown away for Earth's sake. And the payment they had made was not in full. They had given their lives. When their own kind found them and destroyed them they would also have given their bodies. Payment would then be complete.

Not for one moment did he doubt that should he come face to face with one of these three he would shoot him down like a rabid dog, as unhesitatingly as he had shot

Jocelyn Whittingham. It was easier for him than for others to perform such cold-blooded execution; mentally he could *see* the terrible emptiness of the human shell and the thing squirming within.

Three fine young men.

Three rotten apples.

"Damn!" he said loudly. "Damn!"

"What are you cussing over?" inquired Jameson, coming through the door.

"Somebody's sons—and what's been done to them."

"Don't bother your head about them. We've a bigger worry, namely, that of what they're doing to others."

"I know. But it's in my nature to deplore the deplorable." He returned the photographs to the envelope, handed it over. "If I can have copies will you see they're put in my car? They're too large to fold into my pocket."

"We're printing thousands of smaller ones, wallet-size. You'll get a set in due course." Jameson gazed expectantly toward the door. Two men entered. They were young, lean, well-dressed, had an air of quiet competence. Jameson introduced them. "Meet Dan Morris and Bill Rausch. Try getting away from them."

"These are the escort?"

"Yes."

"Hope I won't bore you, boys," said Harper. "Are we ready to go?"

"Right away," Jameson informed. "An army copter is on the roof."

Accompanied by the two silent agents, Harper rode an elevator to its limit, gained the waiting machine, which proved to be a big thirty-seater with port and starboard rotors.

Engines whined into the high note, rotors spun into circles of light. The copter made one small bounce then soared rapidly. At five thousand feet the tail jet spurted flame and sped them westward.

Three and a half hours later they landed in the ornate grounds of a state isolation hospital. An agent met them as they stepped to ground, identified himself as Vern Pritchard.

"You're holding the Whittinghams here?" Harper asked.

"Yes. There are five in the family. They swallowed our story of possible contagion and came without protest. They fear they may be incubating something and can hardly wait to find out."

"None of them have tried to escape?"

"No," said Pritchard.

"Or communicate with somebody at a distance?"

"No."

"Whereabouts are they?"

Pritchard pointed. "In that annex over there."

Gazing meditatively at the place indicated, which was about four hundred yards away, Harper said after a while, "They're okay. You can let them go."

Incredulity came into Pritchard's features as he protested, "But you haven't *seen* them!"

"I don't need to."

"Well, my orders are to be governed entirely by what you say. I take it that you do know what you're saying?"

"I do. I say they're clean. You can release them."

"All right." Hopelessly baffled, Pritchard covered himself against a possible blunder by saying to his fellow agents, "You two are witnesses to this."

They signified agreement, followed Harper back into the copter as Pritchard walked toward the annex. The copter rose, started the return trip.

"Thank the Lord not everyone knows what's wrong with me," remarked Harper, thereby stimulating companion minds into revealing channels.

Mental reactions showed that they didn't know either. Jameson had told them no more than was strictly necessary.

The powers-that-be were trying to hide two menaces from the public, not just one.

Authority was trying to conceal a human pryer as well as an inhuman enslaver. The idea was to use the former to destroy the latter—and then decide the fate of the former.

Chapter 7

Moira stood like one paralysed when he marched surlily into the office, planted himself behind his desk and commenced rummaging through delayed correspondence.

After a while he glanced up and growled, "Well, what's eating you? Have I turned into a purple opprobrium around here?"

"No, Mr. Harper." She sat down weakly, still looking at him wide-eyed. Her ears were perked for sound of oncoming sirens while she wondered how to duck the resulting fracas.

"Don't let your mouth hang open that way. It makes you resemble a half-starved carp. Where's the Pest Control progress-report? They're bellyaching already."

She flew to a cabinet, jerked open a drawer, riffled its cards, extracted one and gave it to him. Her mind was whirly with the belief that she was alone with public enemy number one and somebody ought to do something about it.

"Mr. Riley has been around several times," she informed,

making it sound like a warning and hoping he'd take the hint. "He said he'd call again today."

"He would, the big ugly bum." He studied the card, his expression sour. "Umph! When I say six weeks I mean six weeks and not six days. Dear sirs, in reply to your query of yesterday's date——"

Grabbing her pencil, she scribbled with frantic haste. He spouted another forty words, knew she was making a hopeless mess of her script. He ceased dictating, spoke with a judicious mixture of sorrow and severity.

"See here, Lanky, I am not a convicted criminal. During my absence I have disembowelled none save the few hundred who deserved it. I am not wanted by cops, wardens, army recruiters or the Christian ministry. I am loved only as I have been loved since days of yore. Now pull yourself together and apply your mind to the job. Dear sirs, in reply to your query——"

This time she managed to take it down without error. She slipped paper into her machine, adjusted it, paused expectantly as heavy footsteps approached the office door.

"Here he is," announced Harper, with mock tenseness. "Dive under the desk when the shooting starts."

Moira sat frozen, one finger poised over a key. She dared not look round lest what she saw proved him to be deadly serious. She listened for the faint rustle of clothes indicating that he was drawing his gun.

Next moment Riley bashed open the door in his usual elephantine manner, took the usual two steps to reach the desk. If his scowl had forced his eyebrows an inch lower they'd have served as a moustache. He splayed both hands on the desk while he leaned across it to stare into the other's eyes. Behind him, Moira felt faint with relief, gave the key a tentative tap.

"Now," said Riley hoarsely, "you're going to tell me what the flaming hell is happening right and left. Why are you wanted for murder one moment and not wanted the next?

Why do they list you at top one day and remove you from the bottom another day? Why can't they make up their minds whether you're a hirsute hoodlum or not?"

"Life is just a bowl of cherries. I——"

"Shut up! I haven't finished yet. Why has the F.B.I. emigrated wholesale into this area and calmly confiscated my four best squads? Why have they staked this crummy joint from the roof, the cellars, across the street, up the street, down the street, at both ends of the street and in half a dozen adjoining streets? Why——"

"Why do you turn Moira into a nervous wreck the minute my back is turned?" Harper demanded.

"Me?" Riley fumed a bit. "I never touched her. I'm not that kind. I'm married and happy at it. If she told you I touched her she's a liar. I don't believe she did tell you. You're inventing things in effort to change the subject. But it won't work, see? Why——"

"You looked at her and *thought* things," asserted Harper.

Riley crimsoned and bawled, "All right. I get it. You refuse to talk. You know I can't make you talk. And you're enjoying the situation. It gratifies your simian ego." He let his voice drop a couple of decibels, went on, "Would your lordship grant me the favour of one question? Just one little question, eh?"

"You may voice it," said Harper, trying to be lordly.

"To whom must I go to get the answers?"

"General Conway."

"Jumping Jehoshaphat!" ejaculated Riley. He hitched his pants lest they fall down. "Is it *that* important?"

"Unfortunately, yes. And if they haven't seen fit to give you the details I mustn't do so either. If I told you all I'd usurp authority, and I'm given to understand it's a dreadful thing to usurp authority. It's the unforgivable sin. It breeds anarchy with all its attending features of godlessness, promiscuousness and every form of untaxable naughtiness. Compile your own list——you know more about the wicked."

He reached for another letter from the waiting pile. "Close the door gently as you go out. The glass won't hold under more than another two of your assaults."

"I could assault somebody right now," Riley informed, showing big teeth. "Two burglaries, one hold-up and one case of arson last night. I'm supposed to dismiss them with a light laugh. I'm supposed to concentrate exclusively on looking for three guys named McDonald, Langley and Gould, and do it while robbed of four prowl cars. Nothing else matters but finding a trio of toughies against whom no criminal charge has been entered."

"Nothing else matters," Harper agreed.

Riley leaned closer and whispered, "Be a pal and tell me—what have they done?"

"Ask Conway."

"Thanks for nothing." Riley rattled the glass as he departed.

"Director of Research, Swain Laboratories, Trenton, N.J.," Harper recited while Moira snatched at her pencil. "In response to your inquiry for slow-motion pneumatic micromanipulators suitable for use with type-Z electron microscopes, we have pleasure in quoting for our——" He glanced at the door which had opened. "Well?"

Agent Norris said, "We heard the conversation through the mike. What's that police officer to you?"

"A friend. He thinks he's entitled to my confidence." He sniffed, rubbed his nose, added, "I think so too."

"Why do you say that?"

"I know him of old. He's to be trusted."

"Make note of Harper's friends and intimates," droned Norris's mind, repeating orders in mistaken secrecy. *"They are to be thoroughly checked."* Vocally, he informed, "We let him through to you, being who he is. But we were wondering why he should come out with such peremptory demands for an explanation. What is good enough for the

Commissioner ought to be plenty good enough for him, shouldn't it?"

"He's in a privileged position so far as I'm concerned."

"Are you sure he did not have an ulterior motive in cross-examining you?"

"I did not look to see. I don't peer into everybody's nut, regardless. Besides, I'm busy trying to rescue myself from imminent bankruptcy. What motive could he have?"

"You can guess as well as anyone else—except that you don't have to guess," said Norris. "In a situation such as this it's wise to suspect everyone, including your own mother."

He went out, joined Rausch in the machine-shop. Harper continued with his mail. When lunch-time arrived and Moira had gone out to eat, Harper summoned Norris to the office.

"Moira is a nice girl. She tops me by three inches because I've pulled both her legs so often that they've stretched. But we get along all right."

"What's this to me?" Norris asked.

"I wouldn't like her to get hurt if she was around when a hatchet-man broke in. She's another worm on the same hook and I'm not paying her for taking those risks."

"You're the one who's supposed to warn us of an attack," Norris pointed out. "Without you we're working blind."

"I know. But I'm not holding her hand twenty-four hours per day. Do you suppose it might be best to get rid of her for a while? How about me sending her on paid leave until this affair is over?"

"No. You can play your part only by sticking to normal routine. Make enough changes and a trap starts looking like a trap."

"They might jump her outside, hoping to use her to get at me. It wouldn't work, thank God. I'd know what was coming before it got here. Yet I'd hate to turn the guns on her because she'd ceased to be Moira any more. What's done can't be undone. I'd like to prevent the doing in the first place."

"She must take her chances the same as everybody else," said Norris impassively. "It's no worse for one than for another."

"It is worse," Harper contradicted, "because one's more likely to be picked on than another. I'd be happier if she had a guard, day and night."

"She has. We tied a couple of men on to her at the start. Same applies to your other employees. We've covered all your regular contacts as well. If anyone tries the tactic of approaching you in familiar form they're going to have a hard time finding one suitable and fancy free."

"I could find one any minute," Harper declared.

Norris jerked an eyebrow. "Somebody not under continual observation?"

"Yes."

"Then it's your duty to tell me."

"An agent," said Harper. "Any agent. Who is watching the watchers?"

"That problem is beyond solution. Our men are working in pairs already. We could group them in threes, fours, tens or twenties and find it not enough. The line has to be drawn somewhere between the desirable and the performable. They're operating in pairs, and that makes it impossible for one man to be taken by himself."

"So they must be confiscated two at a time?"

"If that can be done."

"The enemy can do anything that human beings can do. For all I know to the contrary they can also do one or two things that we can't."

"We'll see about that," promised Norris.

The fourth successive day of ordinary, uneventful business routine found Harper bored with playing bait for fish that apparently had ceased to exist. His chosen role didn't seem such a bright idea after all. Perhaps he had based it on a grossly exaggerated sense of his own importance. Perhaps Venusian plans already had developed far enough to remove fear of premature detection. Perhaps they'd become sufficiently well established no longer to care a damn for Harper or any of his ilk.

Meanwhile he had become fed up with being followed wherever he went, finding G-men lounging at every street corner, occupying nearby tables in restaurants, standing beside him in comfort stations, breathing down his neck at the theatre, mooching outside his bedroom night-times. The price of human liberty was to sacrifice his own.

Monotony was broken and faith in his purpose restored when he arrived at the office early, spread the morning paper across his desk and found a news item tucked away at bottom of a column inside.

Savannah, GA. A brief but bloody gun-battle took place near here at midnight when F.B.I. agents raided the Rankovic farm. Two men were killed, four taken into custody. Two more are believed to have escaped. Declining to reveal the purpose of the raid, Area Director Stephen Maddox states that the F.B.I. acted upon direct orders from Washington.

It was a most unusual report in several respects. For one, it had been played down. For another, the precise location was not stated and no names were mentioned other than that of Maddox. Lastly, this fight had occurred when all forces of law and order were engaged in one task and one only. Obviously, therefore, the incident had some bearing on the main issue.

This was confirmed ten minutes later when Jameson phoned long distance. "Seen the news?"

"I've just been reading it."

"It should have been on the dawn radiocast but we kept it off. We're having a heck of a time persuading news services to minimize such items. Naturally they want to know why and we can't tell them."

"What happened?" asked Harper, watching the other's face in the visiscreen.

"I can't say too much even on an officially cleared line. In brief, one of our men picked up Langley's trail, followed it to the Rankovic farm. Langley must have moved out during the short lapse of time between our man's report and the raid. Anyway, we didn't get him. The fox had bolted, leaving the hole still warm."

"More's the pity."

"Two are dead. Their bodies are being shipped out for examination," Jameson went on. "Of the four we captured three emphatically deny that they took any active part in the battle. They say they merely happened to be in the house when the shooting started and took cover until it ended. We've given them the paraffin test and the result is negative."

"What about the fourth?"

"He's brother of one of the casualties. Says he was in bed, woke up when the ruckus started. Pulled on his pants and ran downstairs, joined his brother and another guy in slinging slugs out the windows. He swears that none of them knew they were firing upon the law."

"Sounds plausible," commented Harper.

"He gave up when tear-gas got him. By that time the other two were going cold. All four captives recognize Langley's picture, know nothing about him except that he'd been rooming there a couple of days and left at ten-forty or not much more than an hour before the raid."

"Almost seems as if he'd been tipped off."

"He couldn't possibly have been. He was just plain lucky. Anyhow, I've not called merely to tell you the story. There's more to it than that. When we made the raid we surrounded the place, knocked and demanded entry. Somebody fired back through the door. Therefore, although Langley wasn't present, it made little difference—the house still concealed someone anxious not to be grabbed. What does that suggest to you?"

"Langley had made himself a pal."

"Yes, and he may have made himself more than one. Some fellow named Waggoner pulled out same time as Langley. We know nothing about him except that he and Langley are teamed up. We have a good description and, of course, the search is continuing for both."

"You learned nothing about the other two?" Harper asked.

"McDonald and Gould? No, not in that locality. They appear to have split up. They're trying to make it harder for us by keeping apart." He paused while the screen showed him to be consulting a document below the level of the distant scanner. "I want these four captives put to the test without delay. They may not be what they appear to be."

"Want me to come there?"

"No. It would spoil that set-up at your end. We're flying the four to you. Give them the penetrating eye and say whether they are or they aren't."

"I'll do that."

"Thanks a lot. There's something else too. So far nobody has taken a bite at your buttocks. As you said yourself, it all depends on whether they knew the identity of that girl and whether or not the filling station murder was a coincidence. To date we have no evidence to show that they actually know they're being sought or that they know we have learned of the ship's return. So it's——"

"Has the ship been found yet?" interjected Harper.

"Not a sign of it. It couldn't have been destroyed beyond recognition; a professional breaking-up yard with gas-cutters and furnaces would take a month to get rid of that mass of metal. Latest theory is that it's concealed somewhere in sub-Arctic wastes or has been dumped in the ocean. The latter seems the more likely. In that case the crew must have got ashore by using their rubber raft. We're raking the coasts in effort to discover it."

"Well, it's an idea. What were you saying about nobody biting me?"

"I was pointing out that up to last night they may not have known for sure that the hunt is already in full cry. But the newspaper yap specifically mentioning the Rankovic farm could be a giveaway if Langley reads it. We tried to persuade the press to leave it alone or at least suppress the name of the farm. For our pains we got a bleat about freedom of speech and liberty of publication. There's now a fair chance that the fugitives are no longer basking in a sense of false security. They may look into the question of what ended it and belatedly trace the cause to you. You'd do well to be extra-wary from now on."

"I'll tell Norris," said Harper. "He's my nursemaid."

"There's no need to. If he isn't actually listening-in he'll soon be informed by somebody who is listening. All your calls are being monitored."

"*Solely* as a measure of protection?" inquired Harper.

"Yes," said Jameson, without hesitation. He cut off. The visiscreen clouded, went blank.

"Lousy liar!" Harper glowered at the wall. "They are more bothered about my big ears than my whole skin."

The suspected quartet arrived a few minutes before the office was due to close. Norris lined them up in the machine-shop where they stood manacled together, staring around, openly puzzled by their presence in such a place as this. Half a dozen agents shared their company and watched them narrow-eyed.

Norris went into the office and said, "They're here. How about it?"

"No luck," Harper told him. "They are normal enough to be downright dull."

"Okay." He went out, came back. "I've had three of

them taken away. Jameson wants your report on the remaining guy. He admits taking part in the shooting, claims that he didn't realize what he was doing. Is he telling the truth?"

Shoving aside the papers with which he'd been dealing, Harper appeared to lay back while he pondered the question. He listened, picked up a worry that nagged like toothache but failed to provide an answer. So he probed, drove the mind in the other room away from its present anxiety and on to the recent cause.

"It's true enough. He got a scare that sent him into a panic."

"That's all we want to know."

Harper watched him depart, sighed deeply, slid the papers into a drawer and looked at his watch. It was time to call it a day.

At three o'clock the following afternoon the elusive foe put in its first appearance. Harper was taking it easy just then, his chair tilted on its back legs, his feet on the rim of the desk, his mind wide open as idly he watched Moira sorting invoices.

His mental faculty had two distinct methods of functioning which he liked to symbolize as radio and radar. When he was playing at radio he merely listened and put up with whatever programmes were being broadcast in the vicinity. If he switched to radar he transmitted a pulse of his own which stimulated some other mind into producing a required response.

When he listened he took pot luck, accepted what was being offered whether informative or not, and ninety-nine times out of a hundred it was stuff not worthy of a moment's attention. But when he probed he got what he wanted by nudging the other mind into thinking of it. So far as ordinary human beings were concerned it made not the slightest difference which method he adopted because they were blissfully unconscious of both.

With a Venusian mind it wasn't the same; that had been

his first lesson learned when he contacted the entity owning the Whittingham girl. In some subtle way the Venusians differed. He could listen to one, radio-fashion, without it realizing that it was being overheard. But if, radar-like, he prodded one to compel release of a wanted datum, it felt the prod and took immediate alarm.

Telepathic power had its limitations. None knew that better than he did. Even with normal humans it became frequently necessary to conceal probing under a cloak of speech, to hold conversations spiced with leading questions that would stimulate desired responses. The alternative was to pick up a useless mess of stuff cerebrated at the others' whims.

To deal with a Venusian mind was not as easy. It became doubly difficult when squatting in the middle of an ambush. He could listen in the hope that the prey would betray its own coming but had to be extremely careful about administering a mental jab. To probe too early might result in the other's escape with the news that one or more minds could detect things hidden from a million eyes. To probe too late might bring about a last minute struggle and the death of something they wanted to catch alive.

Right now he was slowly and rhythmically rocking the chair and straining its hind legs which gave forth protesting squeaks. Over the last few days he had not listened continuously. It was impossible to do that and give attention to other matters. Besides, there was no need to do so. It was sufficient for his mind to make a two-seconds sweep around the neighbourhood every couple of minutes, much like a lighthouse beam circling across dark and stormy seas.

He rocked and made his umpteen hundredth or thousandth sweep, ceased punishing the chair, sat erect. Moira glanced at him expectantly, saw that his attention was not on her, resumed her sorting. He listened again to something far away, maybe a thousand yards or more, half-hidden in the general hubbub. It drew nearer, slowly but steadily, at a rate corresponding with walking pace. It was an inhuman mind gaggling like an angry gander.

"Norris!" he yelled.

Moira gave a jerk, dropped a bunch of papers, scrabbled for them on the floor.

The door whisked open and the agent looked in. "What's the matter?"

"I think this is it."

"You mean——?"

"It's coming on two feet. No car. On the sidewalk taking a stroll."

"Stay where you are!" ordered Norris. He bolted from sight.

Going to the window, Harper looked on to the road ten feet below. He opened the casement, leaned out to get a better view. That this made him an excellent target did not worry him in the least; there was no point in them coming after him except to learn his technique—and secrets cannot be extracted from the dead.

If there was one pedestrian in sight there must have been a thousand. The mind he sought had to be among that cluster on the left-hand side of the road between four and five hundred yards to the north. His directional sense assured him of that much but it could not detach one individual from a distant bunch of nondescripts.

Still leaning out and watching, he waited for the weird mind to draw closer. Three hundred yards, two hundred, one fifty. By now he had narrowed the possibility down to three people; a smart housewife tripping along perkily; a plump and prosperous-looking business man in his early forties; a lanky, lantern-jawed individual who slunk along close to the wall.

Behind him, Norris reappeared and said, "All set. Now can you——?"

Ignoring him, Harper made a vicious mental stab along the receiving-line. The result came back in a split second:

intense shock, wild alarm, frantic desire to escape and bear warning elsewhere.

The housewife kept going without faltering or changing pace. The lanky slinker maintained gait and manner. The plump man stopped in his tracks, glared wildly around, swung on one heel and hurried back whence he had come. He moved at a rapid walk, about as fast as he could go without attracting unwelcome attention.

Harper jumped out the window. He heard a gasp from Norris, an exclamation from Moira before he landed heavily. His gun was already in his right fist as he regained balance and plunged forward in the wake of the escapee.

Something in the expressions of passers-by told the quarry that things had begun to happen behind him and now was the time to hustle. He did not bother to look backward for confirmation. Lifting arms to sides he broke into a headlong run. For one of his portly build he showed a remarkable turn of speed.

A bewildered clerk carrying a large box danced in front of the charging Harper who snarled. "Out of my way, Stupid!" then brushed him aside and pounded on. Back of him someone was shouting indistinguishable words in authoritative tones. On the corner six hundred yards ahead someone else blew a shrill whistle. A police car siren started wailing. Two agents stepped out of a doorway ahead of the fugitive, weapons in hands, and bawled an order to halt. Two more came racing down the opposite side of the road.

The plump man wasn't finished yet. Taking as little notice of the guns as one would of peashooters, he dived through the main door of an office building. Harper went in five seconds later, red-faced and breathing hard. Two agents followed close upon his heels. A car squealed into the kerb, unloaded four more.

One of a bank of self-operated elevators was going up fast, taking the fugitive with it. Stopping at its folding gate, Harper scowled upward, watched the other's feet disappear from sight. One pair of agents raced up nearby stairs. Two more jumped into an adjoining elevator and boosted it skyward.

Putting the muzzle of his weapon to the gate's lock, Harper fired, busted it, hauled the gate open and halted the elevator at third floor level. He had hoped to get the quarry stuck between floors but the apparatus proved to be of automatic-levelling type and responded to sudden loss of power by letting its box sink into adjustment.

Listening to the minds above he detected the fugitive's break-out on the third floor, the nearness to him of the agents on the stairs, and knew what was going to happen before he could prevent it.

He galloped up the stairs with sweat beading his brow. He had covered the first flight and half the second, taking steps three at a time, when overhead there sounded a terrific blast, a tinkle of falling glass, a brief pause followed by a hammering burst of explosions. His speed upped itself another twenty per cent while his lungs heaved.

While taking the turn from second to third he heard the yowl of an alien spark becoming extinguished in a useless body, also the wild, despairing cry of something more human on its way out. He slowed, mounting the remaining stairs at normal pace, sadly knowing that he was too late.

The third floor corridor was a shambles. Three agents stood in a little group looking over the scene. One was holding a heavy riot-gun still warm in the muzzle. Another was mopping blood that dripped steadily from his left ear. The third was gazing gloomily at the body of a fourth sprawled near the top of the stairs, crimson splotches on chest and face.

Ten yards from the elevator lay the corpse of the plump man. He was not a pleasant sight. The riot-gun had tried to cut him in half and nearly succeeded. Glass from two broken doors and shattered ceiling lights lay in glittering shards along with flakes of paint and fragments of plaster. One or two scared faces began peeking furtively from doorways farther along. The plump man showed them his ample backside and lay content to bleed.

Chapter 8

The man with the dripping ear bent over the agent supine by the stairs, slid a hand under his vest, felt around and rasped, "He's dead." He stood up, patted a crimson-spotted handkerchief to the side of his head. "If he hadn't beaten me to the top he mightn't have got it. And if I hadn't been four steps lower I'd have got it all over and right through."

"We soared past him in that other box," explained the one with the riot-gun to Harper. "When he stopped so suddenly we overshot him and had to back down. It was just then that he got out and tossed an egg at the other pair. A splinter went right through the floor and between my feet. We jerked open the gate, saw him running down there and gave him a burst before he could throw any more."

A horde came charging up the stairs, Norris and Rausch in the lead. Loud murmurings came from the street far below. Harper realized that he was still gripping his gun, tucked it away.

Norris glanced around, thinned his lips, examined the

agent lying by the stairs. "He looks gone to me. Rush him down to the ambulance, just in case." He turned to the others. "What happened?"

They told him, finishing, "Fat lot of chance we had of taking him alive."

One of the onlookers opened a penknife, picked at the wall, dug out a ragged piece of metal. He studied it closely and said, "Army grenade by the looks of it." He gave the fragment to Norris. "What do you think?"

"Yes, you may be right. We'll have to start checking the armouries. Frisk him and let's see what else he's got."

They made thorough search of the plump man's clothes. No more weapons, not even a vest-pocket gun. The grenade was all he had carried in the way of lethal objects. He had an expensive watch, a diamond stickpin and a well-filled wallet. His clothes were of top quality and his hand-made shoes had cost him plenty. It was pretty obvious that instead of walking down the street he could well have afforded to come along in a private copter and dump himself on Harper's roof.

They laid him flat on his back, revealing a double-chinned and amiable face closely shaven and well cared for. Even now his features wore the expression of one who would not harm a fly—unless it tried to make off with the stickpin. His hands were clean and soft with pink, almond-shaped nails expertly manicured.

Apart from the watch, pin, wallet and two fine linen handkerchiefs he hadn't another thing in his pockets. That was singular: not a driving permit, business card or identity card; no pen, cigarette case, lighter or bunch of keys. His clothes were devoid of a tailor's label; his shoes bore no maker's mark other than that indicating the size. There wasn't a thing by means of which he could be identified quickly.

"More delay," remarked Norris, with bitterness. "It's going to use up valuable time finding out who he is." Again he pawed through the wallet and still found nothing but money, of which there was a sizeable wad. "We must nail him down before we can start the job of tracing all his contacts. He must have been in touch sometime and somewhere—otherwise he wouldn't have run off the rails." He became momentarily hopeful. "I don't suppose *you* can tell us anything about him?"

"Sorry," said Harper, genuinely regretful. It was beyond his power to dig data out of a dead brain. Although he had not had a chance to put it to the test he suspected that a probe might not have forced self-identification from the plump man's living brain. A Venusian involuntarily identifies himself as a Venusian and not as the entity he has usurped. That was the cause of all the trouble, the reason why one exceptional man could recognize them.

"We'll have to do the best we can and do it quickly, too." Norris handed the wallet to an agent. "Make a list of those numbers and have them circulated to the banks fifty miles around. See if anyone has them recorded as paid out and, if so, to whom."

Rausch had opened the watch and examined its insides. He snapped it shut, gave it to another of his men. "This ought to tell us something. It's one of those new-fangled jobs drawing power from variations in barometric pressure. There shouldn't be a million of them around considering what they cost. Find the local distributor. He'll have the movement number on his books and be able to say where it went. Follow it through until you learn who bought it."

The agent took the watch, hastened downstairs.

Studying the stickpin, Rausch said to Norris, "It's a poorer bet but we'll have to take it." He beckoned another agent. "Show it to the leading jewellers. Phone us at once if you trace a sale."

"If his prints are on record we'll know him in a few hours' time," commented Norris, inwardly doubting that they were recorded. "We'll roll a copy and let Washington have a look. Let's hope they've got him on their files.

Somebody had better tote those shoes around town. Any good shoeshop should be able to tell us who makes jobs like those."

"May I see them?" asked Harper. He took them, turned them over and over, doubled them toe to heel and felt their softness and pliability. He handed them back. "Made to measure for him."

Norris nodded, let go a yell of, "Where's the cameraman?"

That worthy appeared, his apparatus dangling from one shoulder. He glanced at the corpse with the professional air of one who had yet to see a stiff with a new shape, size, expression or attitude.

"Tidy his pan and make him look sweet," Norris ordered. "I want a good head and shoulders stereo study to put through the pane. Some gawper might recognize him mooning out of the screen. Give me the pic just as soon as you can have it ready." He turned to Harper. "That's all we can do for the moment. We'll escort you back to your office."

Harper rubbed his chin, looked hesitant, said, "I'm so overawed by surrounding talent that I'm reluctant to offer a suggestion."

"Let's have it," urged Norris.

"You don't mind me amateuring right under your nose?"

"Of course not."

"Well, then," said Harper, "how many grown men go round without even a solitary key in their pockets?"

"That's right. He hasn't a key of any sort. I think he stripped himself of anything he thought likely to give us a lead but he made a sloppy job of it. Or maybe he knew that if anything happened to him it would be enough for him to cause a little delay."

"I also noticed that his right shoe is worn in the centre of the sole," Harper went on. "More worn than is the left shoe." He paused thoughtfully, continued, "And he has the general appearance of a man who had enjoyed prosperity for many years. If he's ever been without a thick wad it was a long, long time ago. Yet he *walked* down the street."

"What are you getting at?"

"Fatty has a car and uses it. His type almost invariably goes in for a big, powerful car the size of an ocean liner. But he didn't employ it this time. Why? Answer: for reasons best known to himself he parked it some place and did the rest on foot. But he did not leave it locked, otherwise he'd have the keys. Why didn't he lock it? Because somebody's sitting in it waiting for him, with the missing keys dangling from the instrument-board. Is that someone still sitting and waiting? Answer: unless he has parked near enough to have seen or heard the ruckus he'll be blissfully ignorant of it."

"Let's go down to the cruiser and put out a radio call. I have enough prowlers to rake the whole area and——"

"Now, now!" Harper chided. "More space, less heed. There are hundreds of parked cars standing around and dozens have people sitting in them. Unless Fatty's playmate happens to be Langley, McDonald or Gould how are you going to spot him?"

"He *may* be one of those three," said Norris, bursting to start the search. "Probably that's why this dead boy walked part of the way. None of those three would risk exhibiting himself near your place in case it was well-covered and he was recognized. He would have to squat out of sight and let a stooge do his dirty work."

"All right. Then I suggest you have all cars make a comb-out for Langley and company, paying special attention to parked jobs with waiting occupants. If the accomplice is not one of those three then he's Mr. Anonymous and your men are out of luck. They wouldn't be able to tell him from Joe Soap even if he were cavorting in his naked pelt."

"But *you* could identify him?"

"Providing I manage to get near enough. You'd better take me on a personal tour of all the parking places within, say, half an hour's walk. Within two miles radius. Fatty wasn't running merely for exercise. He scooted in hope of losing himself a short while until he could make a fast getaway. Ten to one that means he had a car stalled some place."

"I think you may be right," agreed Norris. "Let's go!"

They piled into one of the several cruisers now lined up outside the building. Norris took the wheel, Rausch sat by his side, Harper slumped in the back with another agent. About to start, Norris was struck with a thought, looked over his shoulder at the agent in rear.

"We don't know this area too well. You'd better get out and make room for a local cop who can show us around."

"I can direct you to all the likeliest places," said Harper. "Get going. Take the second turn on the right."

At once they moved off, made the turn, reached a park holding some two hundred cars. The machines stood in neat rows like a parade of hardback beetles. Seven had people sitting inside or lounging near by. Harper made a mental dig at each, picked up no vicious reactions.

"Turn left," he ordered. "There are a couple of small dumps on that road and a big one about a mile up on our nearside."

They trundled along at moderate pace while examining all machines *en route*. Nothing was seen to arouse suspicion and no alarm was sprung.

A mile farther on they reached an underground hiding-place holding more than a thousand cars. Rolling down one of the half-dozen wide entrance-ramps they entered a brightly lit cavern in which concrete pillars soared at intervals from a mass of silent vehicles. An attendant came toward them, his curiosity aroused by sight of a police prowler. Norris dropped his window and stuck a head out to speak.

"Quick!" yelped Harper, sitting up and staring ahead. "There he goes—out the middle exit!"

Norris jumped the car forward, narrowly escaped knocking down the attendant. The car roared along the mainway between packed ranks of its fellows. Overhead lights flashed by faster and faster, receded into the rear distance. Supporting pillars zipped past with enough speed to make them resemble a paled fence. The car's bonnet lifted as they hit the exit ramp. The last light fled by, they shot into daylight and the street.

From the left Harper could still pick up the rapidly fading gobble-gobble-gobble of an agitated brain intent on escaping with what it had learned, namely, that gobblings can be heard.

The siren commenced wailing as they spun off the ramp and started down the middle of the broad street. Traffic scattered, fled to the sides and left a clear road far along which a big black car was hurtling as if driven by a maniac. Holding grimly to the wheel, Norris pressed the accelerator to the floorboard. Rausch felt around under a panel, took out a handmike, held it near to his mouth.

"Black Roadking escaping southward on Bailey Avenue. All cars in region of Bailey Avenue South, Greer Avenue South and Mason Turnpike intercept black Roadking."

"If this loaded heap catches a Roadking it'll be a miracle," Harper observed.

They took no notice. The agent beside him leaned over, tugged a gun from a pocket, held it on his knees.

"Car Forty-One making for Bailey Avenue South," said an impassive cop, speaking out of the instrument board.

Harper squinted ahead, decided they'd lost a couple of hundred yards in less than a mile. He held on as they rocked around a halted bus.

"Car Eleven on Mason," announced another voice.

"Car Four on Mason at Perkins Corner," said a third.

The fleeing Roadking, now visibly diminished by its increased lead, made a sudden swerve as if about to dive up a side road, but at the last moment swerved back, cut the corner and continued down Bailey.

A moment later the reason became evident when a cruiser rocked out of the side road, set after it in hot pursuit. The newcomer was about half-way between Harper's car and the Roadking, made better pace because of its lesser load but still could not gain an inch on the excessively high-powered fugitive.

"What did I tell you?" griped Harper. "Fat men with fat wallets buy fat engines that guzzle a gallon of alk to the mile." He sniffed in disgust, added by way of comfort, "You can't bust his balloons either. Those Roadkings run on sorbo-centred solids."

"Car Twenty-eight at junction of Mason and Bailey."

"That's the spot," gritted Norris. "They'll stop him."

"They'll have to crash him and it'll be a hell of a wallop by the way he's going," said Rausch, holding his mike to one side as he gazed anxiously ahead. "There's no safe way to halt him unless we follow until——"

Taking advantage of the other's preoccupation, Harper leaned forward and bawled into the conveniently held mike. "No half measures! Shoot the bastard!"

"Hey, you!" Rausch snatched the mike away, turned his head to throw a scowl.

In that instant the listening Car Twenty-eight opened fire. The cruiser ahead of Harper's car promptly swung in to the kerb, crawled cautiously forward and gave full view of the second cruiser parked half a mile farther along.

The Roadking whizzed hell for leather past Car Twenty-eight, covered a hundred and fifty yards, yawed wildly twice, made a violent turn that took it over the sidewalk and into a shopfront. The sound of the crash was like an explosion. Haberdashery sprayed outward. An inflated shirt tried to soar across the avenue on flapping arms. Two police officers scrambled out of Car Twenty-eight, raced toward the wreckage.

"That's done it," growled Norris, easing pressure on the

pedal and reducing pace. He snapped over his shoulder at Harper, "Who's running this show?"

"I am. And if you didn't know it before you know it now."

"Our orders are———"

"To blue blazes with your orders," said Harper toughly. "I appreciate your co-operation and sometime or other you're going to appreciate mine."

He opened the door as the car stopped, got out, made for the Roadking knowing in advance that yet again an alien spark had become extinguished within a broken body. But at least no normal human being had been killed—that was one consolation.

In the rear of the shopfront a busted show-robot sprawled over the Roadking's bonnet and leered inanely at the dead driver. The robot wore a tartan hat tilted drunkenly over one eye and the force of the impact had filled its pants with broken parts. The driver sat bowed forward, his face rammed into the wheel, a pair of lurid socks complete with pricetag draped across his neck.

Two police officers waded through smashed glass, torn handkerchiefs and tattered pyjamas, dragged at the car's door. They knocked display-stands out of the way the better to get at it.

Harper was about to join them when a slender individual pranced out of the shop, picked on him with much gesturing of white hands and indignant fluttering of long eyelashes.

"Look at that!" shrilly insisted this apparition. "Just *look* at it! What am I going to do *now*?"

"I could make a suggestion," said Harper, surveying him. "But I don't care to be suggestive."

"This is too bad," insisted the other. "Simply too *too* bad. Somebody will have to pay for it. Somebody———"

"Sue the stiff in the car," Harper told him. "He did it." Joining the police, he helped lug out the body.

The protestor shifted attention to Norris who was following close upon Harper's heels. "Only last night I dressed that window. It's really *sickening*. It makes me so mad I could *spit*. I don't know what——" He broke off and his large eyes went next size larger as they saw the corpse being carried past and laid on the sidewalk. "Why, Mr. Baum!"

"You know this porker?" demanded Norris swiftly.

"Yes, indeed. He's Mr. Baum. Mr. Philip Baum. Only last week I sold him a most fetching line in——"

Staring down at the plump and slightly familiar features, Harper interjected, "Has he a brother?"

"Yes," said the slender man, working his eyelashes and gazing fascinatedly at the dead face. "Mr. Ambrose Baum. A little older. Three or four years, perhaps. Isn't this *awful*? Mr. Baum! My window! Just *look* at it! It makes my stomach turn right over!"

"Where do the Baums live?" asked Norris.

"In Reevesboro. I'd——" He stopped, let his mouth hang open while he looked with horror at the shattered show-robot which slowly slid down from the bonnet and on to its knees, belched loudly, emitted a whirr and two clicks then went cross-eyed. He shuddered at the sight. "Alexander is ruined, completely *ruined*. I'd like to know who's going to compensate for all this."

"Pick on your insurance company," said Norris. "Where in Reevesboro is the Baum house?"

"Somewhere on Pinewalk Avenue, I believe. I can't recall the number. It should be in the phone book."

"Bring out your phone book and let's have a look at it."

"There's no need," put in one of the police officers, searching the body. He straightened up, holding a card. "He's carrying identification. It says he is Philip Kalman Baum of 408 Pinewalk Avenue, Reevesboro. The car is registed in name of Ambrose Baum of same address."

The other officer added, "This one is deader than a mackerel. His chest is shoved right in. The wheel did it."

Norris turned to the agent who had accompanied them

from the beginning. "You take charge here. You know how to handle it. Tell the pressmen nothing. Let 'em yawp—and refer them to our field office." He beckoned to Harper. "We need you along."

Entering the cruiser the three hustled away from the scene around which pedestrians had gathered in a murmuring semi-circle.

"We may want more help than we've got," remarked Norris, driving at high speed. "You'd better cancel that Roadking call and see who's still on the turnpike. Tell them to follow us into Reevesboro."

Rausch found the mike, sent out the message and a voice came back saying, "Car Four on Mason Turnpike at Perkins Corner."

"Pick us up and tail us to Reevesboro," Rausch ordered.

They reached the big twelve-track artery, gained top pace. A green Thunderbug was running ahead of them. They overhauled it slowly, passed, moved ahead. The Thunderbug was being driven by a matronly blonde. Harper stared at her thoughtfully, picked his teeth and said nothing. He was tired of feeling around inside green Thunderbugs.

After four miles a prowl-car shot off the verge and raced behind them. Another six miles and they side-tracked from the turnpike, ran into Reevesboro, found the address they were seeking. It was a small but attractive house standing in a half-acre plot.

Driving a short distance past, Norris stopped, signalled the following car to close up behind. He got out, went to the other car in which were two police and two agents.

He said to the police, "You fellows stay here in case some escapee takes a fancy to an official auto." Then to the agents, "You two get around to the back of that house. If anyone beats it that way as we go in through the front, he's your meat."

"You're wasting time," advised Harper, near enough to the house to know that nothing alien lurked within.

"I'm the judge of that," Norris retorted. He waited for the two agents to make their way round the back, then started toward the front door. "Come on!"

A grey-haired, motherly woman answered the bell. She was in her late fifties or early sixties, had toil-worn hands and meek features.

"This is the Baum house," said Norris, making it a statement rather than a question.

"That's right," she agreed. "But Mr. Philip and Mr. Ambrose aren't here just now. I don't know when they'll be back."

"They'll never be back," Norris told her.

Her wrinkled hand went to her mouth while she gazed at him in thoroughly startled manner. "Has . . . something happened?"

"Unfortunately, yes. Are you a relative?"

"I'm Mrs. Clague, their housekeeper," she informed a little dazedly, "Are they——?"

"Any relatives living here?" interrupted Norris.

"Oh, no. They're confirmed bachelors and have nobody related to them near by. In this house there's only the maid and myself." She swallowed hard. "Are they hurt?—badly?"

"They're dead. We're law officers. We'd like to have a look around."

"Dead?" She whispered it as she stepped backward and let Norris enter with Harper and Rausch following. Her mind had some difficulty in grasping the full import of the news. "Not *both* of them surely?"

"Both, Mrs. Clague. I'm sorry." Norris extracted three photographs from his wallet, showed them to her. "Do you recognize any of these men?"

She blew her nose, wiped her eyes, studied the pictures bemusedly. "No, I don't."

"Sure you haven't seen any of them recently?"

"I'm positive."

"Where's this maid you mentioned?"

"In the kitchen. Do you wish to speak with her?"

"Yes."

She called, "Winnie! Winnie!"

Winnie slouched in, a plump, ungainly girl with the placid eyes of a ruminating cow.

"Know these?" demanded Norris.

She ogled the photographs. "No, sir."

"If any of them had visited recently would you or Mrs. Clague have been sure to have seen them?"

"Uhu. I guess so."

The housekeeper put in, "Mr. Ambrose and Mr. Philip seldom had visitors. They used this house only for relaxation and sleep. And they kept late hours. Two or three o'clock in the morning they'd come home sometimes. But always sober, I'll say that for them. I——"

"What did they do for a living?" Norris asked.

"They have three jewellery shops somewhere or other. And a small wholesale warehouse in town. Their father started the business, I believe. He's been gone a good many years. They were two nice gentlemen and it's terrible to think they're——"

Norris cut the garrulity with an impatient gesture. "We want to look over any papers they've left lying around. Where did they keep their correspondence?"

"All their business files will be at the office," said Mrs. Clague. "But their personal letters will be in that desk or perhaps upstairs in their rooms."

"All right, Mrs. Clague. We're sorry to trouble you but these things happen. If you're not too busy how about fixing some coffee?"

Still somewhat bewildered, she agreed, retreated to the kitchen as if glad to escape their questions. Winnie slopped along behind her, turned twice to look back with a bovine smile before she too disappeared. Norris frowned after her.

"What was that slut smirking at?" he asked.

"You," Harper informed. "She's about I.Q. 70 but that doesn't spoil her appetite for a tasty hunk of man. It's what comes of being a handsome Fed."

"Nuts!" growled Norris, looking sour. He spoke to Rausch. "We've no time for search-warrant formalities and by the looks of it there's nobody around to bawl about the matter. I'll rake through this desk. You give the bedrooms a going-over. When we've finished we'll run into town and frisk the office. We must compile a list of all contacts they've made these last few weeks."

Rausch tramped upstairs, Norris spent five minutes trying to open the desk, failed, called in one of the two agents stationed at back.

"Finaygle this lock for me, Yensen."

Examining it, Yensen went out to the garage, returned with a length of wire. "Another Roadking is stashed in there. Same model and one number higher. They must have bought them together." He fiddled with the wire, turned the lock, rolled up the lid which automatically released the drawers.

Avidly Norris pounced on the contents, pulling documents from pigeon-holes, scanning them rapidly, putting them aside. He lugged out the drawers one by one, found a dull black gun concealed in a camera carton, handed it to Yensen.

"Hang on to that. The ballistics boys may be able to dig some data out of it."

After a while he finished reading the last of a bunch of letters, shoved them back, grunted discontentedly. "Go ask Mrs. Clague when the Baums were last here."

Yensen departed, came back. "She says they had breakfast this morning."

"That's peculiar." He turned to Harper. "All this stuff is chitchat, mostly from friends in the trade. It averages a letter a day. But there's nothing filed for the last five days. If the average was maintained there are five letters missing."

131

"They may be at the office," Harper suggested. "Or——"

"Or what?"

"Maybe they destroyed them on receipt."

"Why should they do that?"

"Because the messages were devoid of interest, they having become alien to the readers."

"We'll check at their office before we jump to any conclusions," Norris decided. "Either they kept them or they didn't."

"If a search elsewhere fails to produce them we can bet on two things," said Harper. "Firstly, that the Baums were taken over about five days ago. Secondly, that the enemy is no longer so desperate to get established in number and is starting to be choosy."

"How d'you make that out?"

"The Baums have been in daily contact with Mrs. Clague and Winnie. We know that much. But neither of the women were touched. They've been left alone despite that they're easy prey. They've lived with the Devil but retained their souls. Aren't they the luckiest people?"

"You give me the creeps," Norris complained. He turned to Yensen. "Make a list of names and addresses from this correspondence and bring it to H.Q. We'll have to follow up every one of them."

Rausch reappeared saying, "Nothing of any significance up there except a couple of telephone numbers scribbled on a pad by the phone in Ambrose's room."

"We'll look into those later." Norris had a final, dissatisfied glance around, saw nothing of fresh interest. "If the fate of the Baums isn't yet known to those we're seeking you can see what's likely to happen. Somebody's going to come along wanting to know how the brothers made out. If all of us go to their office there will be nobody here to make a grab. We'll have to stake this place until the news gets out and warns off possible visitors."

"I'll stay with Yensen," Rausch volunteered. "If any-body——"

Something went *whirr-whirr* above.

"The phone!" yelped Norris.

He charged upstairs, taking steps two at a time. The others crowded behind him. Entering Ambrose's room he eyed its bedside phone warily.

"Notice any other telephone here?"

They shook their heads.

"Too bad. No chance of holding the caller while we trace him." Extracting his pocket handkerchief he draped it over the tiny scanner then lifted the earpiece. The small visiscreen at once lit up but revealed no picture. That meant a similarly obscured scanner at the other end. "Hello!" he said.

"Var silvin, Wend?" demanded a voice bearing the sharpness of deep suspicion.

"Baum residence," said Norris, frowning. "Can I help you?"

Click! The line went dead. Norris rattled the instrument, raised the operator, identified himself. "Where did that call originate? Let me know quickly—it's urgent!" He hung on for most of a minute, listened again, snorted, racked the phone and told the others, "The Baum warehouse. Evidently they had a rendezvous there with somebody who got worried and called after they'd failed to turn up. We missed a trick by not finding out the place and going there first."

"Get along right now," urged Rausch. "I'll stay with Yensen, just in case."

Norris nodded, signed to Harper and they hastened to the car. Ordering one of the waiting police to join them, he drove away at top pace.

"You might as well take it easy," advised Harper, with unconcealed pessimism. "There'll be nobody at the place. Whoever hangs up on a call isn't going to sit around."

"That's what I think," agreed Norris, maintaining speed. "But if we fail to catch somebody it won't be for lack of trying." He used a hand to indicate the microphone under the dashboard. "Put out a shout. Any cars near the warehouse to go there at once. Detain anyone found on the premises."

Harper did as told. Two voices answered, said they'd be there within a couple of minutes.

"A couple of minutes too late," he commented, replacing the mike.

Chapter 9

The warehouse proved to be an ancient but solid redbrick building with six heavily barred and shuttered windows and a cumbersome steel door. It had the appearance of property once designed to hold merchandise regarded as a chronic temptation to the backward neighbourhood. Two cars were lined up outside and three police were standing defeatedly near by.

"We've three men waiting around the back," one of them told Norris. "The place is locked. Nobody answers the bell. No sounds inside. Looks like it's empty."

"Then we'll break through the door."

It took some time to do that but they managed without overmuch damage. Not a soul lurked within. The first floor held a number of flat glass showcases exhibiting junk jewellery arrayed on black velvet. The floor above was littered with light crates and cardboard cartons, some full, some empty. A small office of clapboard and plastiglass stood in a corner.

Entering the office, Norris moved carefully around, said to one of the police, "Fetch the fingerprint man. Given enough luck we may be able to discover who was waiting here." To Harper he added, "It takes a professional criminal to wipe a place clean of prints—and the characters we're after don't fall into that category."

He went to the desk, slid out its drawers. The contents were not enlightening, mostly billheads, invoices and other business items. A metal filing cabinet proved no more informative.

"Tell you one thing," remarked Harper, sniffing the air. "The Baums and their associates seem fond of cold-cure."

"What makes you say that?" asked Norris.

"Ambrose had a faint odour. So did Philip. And I can smell it again here."

Norris twitched his nostrils a couple of times. "Your sense of smell must be a deal sharper than mine."

"People vary that way. So do dogs. I can detect it all right. And I know what it is."

"What is it?"

"Eucalyptus."

"Well, that's mighty useful," commented Norris sardonically. "Now all we need do is track down somebody stinking of eucalyptus."

"You could do worse," Harper opined. "Three smellers in a row, and in one day, means something. Like tobacco. If I'm in a deep forest and smell burning tobacco I know a man is somewhere near."

"So——?"

"Maybe somebody *likes* eucalyptus."

"You come up with the damnedest ideas," said Norris.

"They've got to come from somewhere if we're going to make any progress at all." Harper shoved hands deep in pockets, gazed moodily around. "Anyway, why shouldn't certain people have a craving for the stuff? Koala bears dote on it, so I'm told."

"They eat the leaves," Norris informed. "Besides, we're not trying to cope with koala bears. We're in pursuit of things with bigger teeth and claws."

"So what? Even tigers have fads."

Norris frowned at him, reached for the telephone, handling it delicately so as not to spoil any latent prints. He dialled, spoke to someone.

"This is no more than a wild guess but you'd better note it: check all suspects for an odour of eucalyptus." He racked the instrument, admitted, "It would sound silly to me if this entire business wasn't so crazy."

"Not being a full-time Sherlock," said Harper, "I tend to miss things that are obvious to you but spot others that you may overlook. For instance, what's the scientific conclusion to be drawn from a liking for eucalyptus?"

"I don't know."

"That elsewhere the natural prey is vegetarian and feeds on aromatic shrubs, its favourite food being something akin to eucalyptus. So here the host feels a need born of centuries of conditioning. In other words, they've found a local drug that reminds them of home, sweet home."

"What the devil are you talking about?"

"Sorry, I forgot you've been told only part of the story," said Harper. "You've got to know the whole of it to guess the way I'm guessing."

"Eucalyptus isn't a drug," declared Norris, baffled.

"Not to us, it isn't. God knows what it is to some other guppies."

"Look, did you sniff the stuff when you shot that girl?"

"No, I didn't go near enough or hang around long enough. Her case being the first, I was in a jam, had to get out fast, had no time or inclination to look for what I suspect only now."

"Humph!" Norris thought a bit, resorted to the phone again, called the Baum house, spoke to Rausch. "We're out of luck here. The bird had flown." He listened to some

137

comment from the other end, then continued, "Harper smells eucalyptus, says the Baums smelled of it too. I didn't notice it. Did you?"

Rausch said, "Yes. But I thought nothing of it."

Cutting off, Norris observed, "I should have my nasal passages irrigated."

"This is important," Harper pointed out. "Ambrose and Philip carried the odour. Whoever was here reeked of it. Maybe they stumbled across the stuff with the same glee as a bunch of hopheads discovering a field of Mexican hemp. If so, they'll pass the news one to another."

"Well?"

"The habit will hand humanity a small advantage. If you can't tell what's going on in a suspect's mind you can at least smell his breath." He thought again, added, "By 'you' I mean the forces of law and order in general. *You* couldn't smell an overheated goat under your own bed."

"Thanks for the criticism," grunted Norris. He lapsed into silence as the fingerprint man arrived and set about his business. The newcomer raised prints all over the place, most of them undoubtedly being those of the Baum brothers. When he had finished, Norris ordered, "Get them checked as quickly as possible and let me know the results." He turned to Harper. "Momentarily we're stalled. Let's get back to your office."

"And put the worm on the hook once more, eh?"

Norris glanced at his wrist-watch. "I don't think so. It's a bit too late to expect further action there. You'll be just in time to lock up and go home. If anyone else comes after your blood before tomorrow it's likeliest to be while you're in bed."

"That idea makes for peaceful sleep."

"Don't worry. You're well guarded around the clock."

"I know. Too well for my liking. By the looks of it I'm going to have official company for the rest of my natural life."

"Oh, I wouldn't say that," opined Norris. "This rigmarole is only for the duration of the emergency."

"So it is alleged," Harper grumbled. "But higher up are a few authoritative coots who resent the unalterable facts of life. They're not above replacing one emergency with another so long as it suits their power-game to do so."

He got into the car, sat alongside Norris and returned to the office in silence. He was grouchily aware that when the present crisis ended—if ever it were ended—he would then have the problem of how to get authority off his neck and for keeps.

It wasn't going to be easy.

Morning brought news. Norris poked a head into the office, beckoned him away from Moira's hearing.

"Things are beginning to break," he announced. "Firstly, there were two calls to the Baum house during the night. The caller hung up immediately Rausch answered. Both calls emanated from public booths. That means the Baum's contact man is still in town someplace."

"Assuming there's only one of them," said Harper. "For all we know, there may be a dozen."

"Perhaps. Anyway, we got identifiable prints out of that warehouse office. They are McDonald's."

"Ah! So *he* was waiting there?"

Norris nodded. "We missed him by minutes. Further, we've found that he palled on with the Baums in an hotel one evening. He left with them in Ambrose's car and hasn't been seen since. Two waiters and a barkeep have identified his picture."

"When did he pick them up?"

"Six days ago."

"Just the time we estimated," Harper remarked.

"We're searching the locality for him right now," Norris continued. "If he's still here today we'll find him."

"That may prove more difficult than you expect."

"Why?"

"He doesn't have to stay at an hotel or roominghouse. So you'll gain little making the rounds of those. He doesn't have to rent a flat. He doesn't have to sleep out in the open."

"Then what does he do?"

"He lives in a private house, as one of the family—having *made* himself one of the family." Harper eyed him sceptically. "How are you going to search several thousand private homes?"

"We won't try. There are quicker ways of picking up leads."

"How?"

"Every street has its gossip, its incurable snoop. We have enough photos of McDonald to check with every nosey-parker for miles around. What's more, he can't operate while sitting in a back room behind drawn curtains. He has to emerge sometime. If it was he who called Rausch he went outside his hole-up to do it. He took a risk and was mighty lucky not to be recognized."

"How about sounding the drugstores for abnormal sales of eucalyptus?"

"We've thought of that. Four agents are on the job."

The phone shrilled in the office. Moira picked it up, called to them, "It's for Mr. Norris or Mr. Rausch."

Norris went inside, listened for a while, came back and said to Harper, "That was Jameson."

"Anything new?"

"Yes. Langley's dead."

"So they caught up with him?"

"He was spotted in a stolen car at dawn. Two men were with him, Waggoner and a fellow now known to be a certain Joe Scaife. They ran up against a road-block, abandoned the car and took to the woods. Police, agents and national guardsmen dived in after them. Jameson says they put up such a desperate fight it proved impossible to take them alive. Langley and Scaife were shot dead. Waggoner used his last bullet on himself. That was about an hour ago. Their big problem now is what to tell the newshawks."

"This looks bad to me," Harper admitted.

"Bad isn't the word for it," said Norris seriously. "Waggoner's deed speaks for itself. If these reactions are any criterion we're up against a crazy crowd who'd far rather be killed than caught."

"The Baums behaved the same way," Harper reminded. "The death-before-dishonour touch."

"It's inhuman."

"Of course it is! Get it into your head that we are fighting against mentalities with standards far different from yours and mine. To them, capture may seem a fate considerably worse than death. If so, it wouldn't be enough for us to try to win a battle. More is needed. We must also prevent a last-minute suicide to get one of them alive."

"Our orders are to take them alive at all costs."

"Easier said than done."

"Well, you're supposed to be an ace in the pack," Norris pointed out. "How would you go about it if you happened to find one of them, McDonald for instance?"

Harper mulled the problem, then said, "The all-important thing would be not to let him realize or suspect that he'd been tagged. I don't see anything else for it but to sit around in patience and wait a chance to knock him unconscious or pin him down before he could make a move."

"That comes well from the man who got Ambrose Baum on the run."

"I had to make him react to find out who was which. Up to that point there was no telling with such a crowd in the road. We knew nothing about him until then. McDonald's different. We do know what he looks like. We don't have to kick his breeches to make him betray himself. His face is sufficient giveaway."

"True enough."

"If it comes to that," Harper went on, "and I could organize things my own way—which unfortunately I can't—I would not try to take McDonald alive or dead. I'd let him run free."

"Why?"

"So that he could lead me to others."

"He wouldn't play sucker for long," Norris scoffed. "If you think you could exploit him for months, you're mistaken."

"For what reason?"

"Because it's no darned use him leading you to others unless you profit by it. Therefore you'd have to grab them sooner or later. And directly his contacts start disappearing he'll take alarm, scoot out of sight or blow his head off." Sniffing his disdain of amateur tactics, he finished, "If we can capture him unscratched and intact he'll do all the leading we require and whether he likes it or not. We'll see to that!"

"Have it your own way." Harper returned to his office, saying, "I'm going to carry on with business, otherwise it will never get done." He squatted behind his desk, spent half an hour considering a large blueprint, then gave ten minutes to the long letter that had come with it. "All right, Moira, wet your pencil and be careful with the big words. I——"

Norris looked in and commanded, "Put your hat on. You're wanted again."

"Oh, not now, surely?" growled Harper. "I've important work to do."

"You bet you have," agreed Norris. "But you can't do it there. Hoist your buttocks and come along."

Throwing him an ugly look, Harper said to Moira, "Much more of this and you can have the business as a gift, you being the only one left to cope with it unchivvied."

"Hurry up!" urged Norris. "Never mind the gripes."

Harper did as bidden, went out, followed him down to the car, clambered in.

"They think they know where McDonald has hidden himself," Norris explained.

After a brief run the car halted at one end of a long, tree-lined road sided by tidy bungalows. No other official cruisers were in sight as Norris pointed through the windshield and spoke.

"It's a pink-washed house half-way down on the left. The boys are keeping clear of it so as not to raise an alarm. We'll roll casually past. Take a look as we go by and tell me what you think."

He shifted into gear and let the car move forward at modest pace. They trundled by the pink house which had a close-clipped lawn in front, a locked garage at one side. Nobody could be seen about the place, nobody maintaining a lookout from a window. Reaching the end of the road, Norris parked by the kerb.

"What's the verdict?"

"Nothing doing."

Norris registered acute disappointment. "Are you sure of that?"

"We'll circle around and try again if you're not satisfied."

They circled.

"Nothing doing," repeated Harper. "For all I can tell the house is empty." He glanced at the other. "How did you get a line on this address?"

"One of our agents went the rounds of the taxi companies on the theory that if it was McDonald who made those calls to the Baum house he did not walk to or from the booths. The agent found a driver who recognized McDonald's picture, claimed to have picked him up after midnight and run him to this place."

"After which McDonald walked around the corner and made for wherever his sanctuary really is," Harper suggested.

"The driver saw him use a key and go in. That's likely enough. After all, McDonald isn't a hardened crook, wise

143

in the ways of the underworld. He would be naïve enough not to think of a taxi-trace."

"That's so. Anyway, all I can tell you is that he isn't there at this moment. Maybe he's in my office making preparations for my return. Moira wouldn't like that. Let's go back."

"Bide your time," Norris ordered. "Your correspondence can wait. It'll have to wait. It'll wait a hell of a while when you're dead, won't it?"

"I'll worry none at that stage. I don't have to eat when down the hole."

Taking no notice, Norris pondered a moment, decided, "I'll take a chance on setting off the alarm." Turning the car round, he drove to the house standing next to the pink one. A middle-aged woman was at the door watching him. He beckoned to her and she crossed her lawn, examined him with beady-eyed curiosity. "Can you tell me who lives next door?" he asked, pointing.

"Mr. and Mrs. Reed," she informed.

"Nobody else?"

"No. They have no family. They're not the kind who would, I reckon." She thought again, added, "They've a nephew staying with them just now. He's from someplace out west, so I've heard."

"Would this be the nephew?" inquired Norris, showing her McDonald's photograph.

"Yes. Only he looks a bit older than that."

Norris took in a deep breath. "How long has he been rooming there?"

"About a week." She reconsidered, went on, "Yes, I first saw him last Thursday." Her sharp eyes studied his plain clothes, had a look at the car. Her mind showed her to be impressed by Norris's official tones. "Are you police?"

"If we were we'd have said so," Norris evaded. "We just want to make sure of the Reeds' address."

"That's their house all right," she confirmed. "But you

won't find anyone in. They took their car out this morning and haven't come back."

"About what time did they leave?"

"Eight o'clock. And they were in a real hurry, I can tell you that."

"Don't happen to know where they've gone, do you?" put Norris, with faint hope.

"Oh, no. They said nothing to me, and I didn't ask. I mind my own affairs and leave other people to mind theirs."

"Quite proper of you," said Norris. "I suppose there's nothing for it but to come back later when they're in."

"Heaven knows when that will be," she volunteered. "They took a lot of luggage with them. It gave me the idea that they were going for quite a piece. Not that it's any business of mine, of course. But sometimes one just can't help noticing things."

Norris considered this evidence of her ability to mind her own affairs, then asked, "Have they any friends locally who might put us in touch with them?"

"Not that I know of," she answered. "Those Reeds aren't overly sociable and became even less so after that nephew arrived. In fact if you ask me, they've been downright surly these last few days. Wouldn't speak unless spoken to and then said no more than they could help. Acted as if I were a complete stranger to them, me who's lived next door for twelve years. It made me wonder what on earth had come over them. That nephew had something to do with it, I'm sure."

Harper put in, "Who told you that he was their nephew?"

"Mrs. Reed," she informed. "I said to her, 'Who's the young man?' and she gave me a sharp look and snapped, 'Just a nephew.' You'd have thought I'd asked her for the loan of a hundred dollars from the way she spoke. Naturally I didn't mention him again. I know when to keep my mouth shut."

"Thanks for the information," said Norris. He got the

car going while she remained on the lawn and showed deep disappointment at giving so much and learning so little.

"If that female minds her own business," remarked Harper as they rounded the end corner, "how much might we get out of someone who doesn't?"

Norris grunted and offered no comment.

"What do you propose to do about McDonald?" Harper pursued. "Are you going to stake this place as thoroughly as you've staked mine?"

"It has been watched continually since nine o'clock, but evidently we started an hour too late. And although you saw no sign of the fact, it's still under observation." He weaved the car through traffic, went on, "First thing is to get the tag-number of the Reed car from the vehicle registration bureau and put out a general call for it. The second step is to have that house searched on some pretext or other. The third is to find how and where McDonald picked up the Reeds and, more importantly, whether he's had contact with anyone else beside the Reeds and the Baums. Lastly, I want to know how he's managed to smuggle himself out of this area seeing that all routes are sealed."

"Maybe he isn't out of the area. Maybe he is hidden somewhere near by."

"We'll soon learn." He drove another mile, asked, "Well, what are you thinking about?"

"Langley's dead. McDonald's not too far away and now being sought."

"What of it?"

"Strange that there's not been a whisper about the third fellow, Gould."

"No, there hasn't," Norris admitted. "He appears to have vanished into thin air. That proves nothing except that luck runs better with some than with others."

"If it is luck."

"What do you mean?"

"It doesn't have to be luck. Perhaps he is the cleverest

of the three, a really crafty character. If so, he is also the most dangerous."

"He'll fall over his own feet eventually," Norris assured. "They always do!"

"I've been the subject of a nation-wide hunt myself," Harper pointed out. "Admittedly it wasn't so urgent and intensive. But I had to jump around plenty to stay free. I know what it means to be on the run, which is more than you do, always having been the chaser and never the chased. The man who can disappear like Gould is good. He's too good for comfort."

"That won't save him for ever."

"We haven't got for ever. Time is running short. Every day, every hour counts against us." He shoved open the door as they halted at their destination. "You know only as much as they've seen fit to tell you. I'll tell you something more."

"What's that?"

"If progress proves too slow for success, if we're compelled to face defeat, you'll have another bird's egg in your mental nest before the new year. You'll be really cuckoo in a new and novel sense of the term. Just like everyone else. At least you'll be in the fashion—when it's the latest thing to be one of the walking dead!"

Chapter 10

Business was stalled yet again first thing the next morning, and before he had time even to look through the mail. He arrived at the office, having been tailed by his escort all the way from home, removed his hat and made ready to sling it on to a hook.

"Don't let go," advised Norris. "Haul it back and stick it on your head. You're departing right away."

"Where to?"

"I don't know. They haven't seen fit to confide in me."

That was true enough. Norris's mind held no more information than that an official car had arrived to take Harper some place else, that he would be away the full day and that the guard was commanded to maintain its watch on the plant during his absence.

Harper did not argue the matter this time. Reluctantly he was becoming resigned to the situation. Replacing the hat, he went outside, entered the car in which sat only a driver.

As they moved off a second machine bearing four men

148

followed close behind. Harper waved a satirical goodbye to Norris, who was standing on the sidewalk trying to puzzle out the reason for this peremptory removal of the bait from the trap. Around the corner a third car suddenly pulled out from the kerb and took the lead. This one also held a hard-looking quartet.

"Quite a cavalcade," Harper remarked. "Somebody is according me the importance I've long deserved."

The driver made no response, concentrated solely on following the car ahead. He was a beetle-browed individual of the type that doesn't know the meaning of fear—or any other words. To the rear the third vehicle kept a careful twenty yards distant.

"A hundred dollars if you step on it and lose the entire bunch."

No reply. Not so much as a smile.

Giving it up, Harper slumped in his seat, half-closed his eyes while his mind felt around like invisible fingers. His own driver, he found, knew nothing except that he must keep on the tail of the leading machine, be prepared for trouble and on no account face it if he could run out of it.

The fingers explored farther.

Those in the leading car knew where the procession was heading. And from that moment, so did Harper. He mulled the new-found knowledge a minute or two, dismissed the purpose as something he would learn in due course, gazed idly through the door-glass at passing shops and pedestrians. With habit born of the last few days he made a mental sweep of the neighbourhood every now and again.

They had passed through two sets of traffic lights and over a dozen cross-streets when alien impulses reached him, weak with distance but discernible. Something high up that side-road, six, eight or maybe ten hundred yards away. Something that flashed pseudo-human thoughts in spasms with gigglings and gobblings between.

He sat up red-faced and snapped, "Quick! Turn up there!"

Beetle-brows firmed his thick lips, gave a warning toot on his horn and speeded up. Two faces peered through the rear window of the car ahead which likewise increased its pace. They whizzed across the road without turning and continued straight on.

"You're too slow to keep up with your own boots," commented Harper, sharp-eyed and still listening. "Take this next turn. Make it fast. We can buzz round the block and get him before he fades out."

The car plunged on. It ignored the turn and the next and the next. The faraway squirming mind thinned into nothingness and was lost.

"You bladderhead!" swore Harper. "You've missed a prize chance."

No retort.

He gave it up, lapsed into ireful silence, wondered whether the brief emanations he'd picked up had come from McDonald himself or from yet another of his unsuspected dupes. There was no way of telling. Such minds do not reveal themselves in terms of human identity. All that could be said for certain was that a mortal enemy wandered loose despite that the whole town was beginning to resemble an armed camp.

Surliness remained with him two hours later when the cars rolled through a strongly guarded gateway in a heavily fenced area, went over a small hill and stopped before a cluster of buildings hidden from sight of the main road. A painted board stood beside the main entrance.

DEPARTMENT OF DEFENCE
Biological Research Laboratories

The four from the pilot car escorted him through the doors in the wary manner of men convinced that given half a chance he would take wings and fly. More people given only part of the story and exaggerating the rest, he decided.

He took a chair in the waiting-room and sat, watched by

three of them while the fourth went in search of someone else. In due time the latter returned with a white-coated, grey-haired individual who registered prompt surprise.

"Wade Harper! Well I'm blessed!"

"What's dumbfounding about it?" growled Harper. "You weren't soul-shaken last time we met, four years back."

One of the escort chipped in, saying, "If you and Doctor Leeming already know each other you don't need an introduction. So we'll get along." He went out, taking the others with him.

Leeming explained, "My instructions are to make a check with the help of a specialist who would be brought here this morning. I am given to understand that what he says must be treated as decisive. The specialist's identity wasn't revealed." He backed off a short way, looked the other up and down. "And it's you. Four years haven't done you any good. You look older and uglier."

"So would you if you were in my breeches." Harper gave a sniff of discontent, went on, "I came like royalty, under strong protection. Toughies to the front of me, toughies to the back of me, and for all I know there was a fleet of helicopters parading overhead. All that rigmarole wasn't so you could hand me another problem about how to shave the whiskers off a bacillus. Moreoever, my mercenary instinct tells me you aren't aiming to give me a repeat order for twelve thousand dollars' worth of apparatus. So what's this all about?"

"I'll show you." Doctor Leeming beckoned. "Come along."

Taking him through a series of corridors, Leeming conducted him into a long room cluttered with scientific glassware, stainless steel instruments and, Harper swiftly noted, a few silk-lined cases of his own especial products. A young man, white-coated, bespectacled and serious, glanced up nervously as they entered.

"My assistant, Doctor Balir," introduced Leeming. "Meet Wade Harper." He gestured toward a nearby micromanipulator and its array of accessories. "He's the fellow who makes this stuff."

Balir looked suitably impressed, said, "Glad to know you."

"Then you may number yourself among a select few," Harper responded.

"Take no notice," Leeming advised Balir. "He says the first thing that pops into his head."

"Hence the general ruckus," commented Harper, "seeing what's been popping of late." He stared around. "Well, why am I here?"

Leeming went to a large cabinet, took from it a photograph blown up to full-plate size, handed it over for inspection. It showed a fuzzy white sphere with a band of slight discoloration across its middle.

"A picture of the planet Jupiter," Harper hazarded, momentarily too preoccupied to check his guess by mental probing.

"On the contrary," informed Leeming, "it is something far smaller, though massive enough as such things go. That's an electron-microscope's view of a protein molecule."

"If you want to dissect it you're right out of luck. I can't get down to any method of handling things *that* tiny."

"More's the pity," said Leeming. "But that's not what we're after."

Returning the photo to the cabinet, he turned to a heavy steel safe set in the wall. Opening it carefully, he took out a transparent plastic sealed container in which was a wadded test-tube one quarter filled with a clear-colourless liquid.

"This," he announced, "is the same thing multiplied a millionfold. Does it mean anything to you?"

Harper peered at the fluid. "Not a thing."

"Consider carefully," Leeming advised. "Because to the best of our belief this is still alive."

"Alive?"

"By that, I mean potent. It is a virus extracted from the brainpans and spinal cords of certain bodies."

"A recognizable virus?"

"No."

"Filterable?"

"We did not attempt to filter it. We isolated it by a new centrifugal process."

"Then if it's not dead it's still dizzy from being whirled," said Harper. "Let me try again when it has come to its senses."

"Ah! That's precisely what we want to know. *Has* it any senses? My information is that you, and you alone, can tell us." He frowned and continued, "I have my orders which say that it is for you to pronounce the verdict. If you say that this virus is innocuous, it means either that it has been rendered so by processing and isolation or, alternatively, that we're on the wrong track and must start all over again."

Harper said, "Anyway, you don't have to stand there holding it out at arm's length like a man who's just dug up a dead cat. Put it back in its coffin and screw down the lid. It will make not the slightest difference to my ability to weigh it up. If that stuff were willing and able to advertise its suspected nature I could have told you about it in the waiting-room without bothering to come this near."

Doing as bidden, Leeming fastened the steel safe, spread expressive hands. "So we're no farther than at the beginning?"

"Not necessarily," Harper replied. Leaning against a lab bench, he put on a musing expression while he picked the minds of both Leeming and Balir. Then he said, "You've been told that three space-explorers have returned from Venus afflicted with a possessive disease which is spreading. They have sent you bodies of known victims, starting with a girl named Joyce Whittingham. Your job is to isolate what's doing it, learn its nature and, if possible, devise a cure."

153

"Correct," admitted Leeming. "It's top secret information. Evidently you've been given it too."

"Given it? I took it with both hands. And it was like pulling teeth." Harper leaned forward, eyed him intently. "Are you positive that you have extracted the real cause in the form of that virus?"

"I was fairly certain—until your arrival. Now I'm not."

"What made you so sure?"

"No words of mine can tell you how thoroughly we've dealt with those corpses. The task was made doubly difficult by virtue of everything having to be handled remotely, with every possible precaution against direct contact and contamination. We've had our leading experts on the job twenty-four hours per day and they've done it down to the last fragment of flesh, blood, bone, skin and hair. All we've got to show for it is a formerly unknown virus. That could be it. That should be it." He paused, finished, "But, according to you, it isn't."

"I haven't said so."

"You said it meant nothing to you."

"Neither does it—in its present state." Harper hesitated, continued, "I have the peculiar power to recognize persons afflicted with this disease. If they've not told you how I can do it, I cannot either. Call it another top-secret. The damn world's getting crammed with top-secrets. However, I can tell you one thing."

"What's that?"

"I recognize the symptoms. You're asking me to put a finger on the cause. It's not the same thing, not by a long chalk. So far as I'm concerned it's a quite different problem."

"Well, can you help with any suggestions?" asked Leeming.

"I can give you my ideas. It's up to you to decide whether they make sense or nonsense."

"Let's have them. We need every angle we can get."

"All right. Understand that I'm not criticizing you people in any way when I say that I think the authorities rushed me here because they'd jumped to a silly conclusion."

"What conclusion?"

"That you can undress when you're stark naked. That you can swim without water. That you can pedal down the road without a bicycle between your legs."

"Be more explicit," Leeming suggested.

"You can't be a disease when you've nothing to work upon. You can't run without legs, talk without a mouth, think without brains. If that stuff is what you believe it to be, and what for all I know it really may be, it's hamstrung, tied up, fastened down, gagged and slugged. It is therefore no more than what it appears to be, namely, a dollop of goo. Its power, if any, has ceased to be actual and become only potential. I can detect an actuality. But I can't sit in judgment upon potentiality any more than I can read the future."

"I see what you mean." Leeming put on a slow smile. "You don't give us credit for overmuch intelligence, do you?"

"I haven't defined you as stupid. I'm merely theorizing about my own ability to help."

"All right." Leeming waved a hand toward the steel safe. "That's not all we've got. It's only half of it. We used the rest for a time-honoured purpose: we tried it on the dog."

"You mean you've actually squirted it into someone?"

"Yes, a dog, as I've just said."

Harper gazed at him defeatedly. In all his life he had never picked up a thought radiating from any of the lower animals. Telepathically, the dogs and cats, the birds and bees just did not exist. They cerebrated somewhere above or below the human waveband. He could no more listen to their minds working than he could see beyond the ultra-violet.

"What's happened to it?"

"It lived. It's still living. Like to see it?"

"Yes, I would."

The dog proved to be a black Labrador retriever imprisoned in a heavy cage apparently commandeered from a circus or from some nearby zoo. The cage had a steel floor, heavy steel bars on all sides and across the top, also a sliding mid-gate by means of which the animal could be pinned in one half of its quarters while the other half was being cleaned, its food and water bowls replenished. The Labrador looked incongruous and not a little pathetic in surroundings formidable enough to hold an irate rhinoceros.

Noticing the approaching pair, the dog turned to face them, pawed at the bars, wagged its tail vigorously and emitted a pleading whine. A perfect picture of canine friendliness, it concentrated its attention particularly upon Harper, subjecting him to all the appeal of a pet-shop pup begging to be bought.

"Any comments?" inquired Leeming.

"If appearance is anything to go by, you injected it with nothing more dangerous than dill-water."

"Within the limits of that condition, I agree. But can we place faith in appearances? You've said that you can recognize an actuality. Well, this dog is actual enough. So what is your diagnosis?"

"I can't give one," said Harper. "It's no use me trying to smell out witches among the canine species. My power functions only with respect to a two-legged creature very much like myself but less hairy."

"H'm!" Leeming eyed the Labrador which now was standing on its hind legs, forepaws against bars, and openly inviting Harper to take it out for a walk. He frowned deeply, said, "Notice how all its attention is on you and how it is ignoring me?"

"That's natural. I'd prefer me to you if I were a dog."

"I'm not joking," Leeming assured. "I'm deadly serious."

"Why?"

"We shot a dose of virus into that animal at noon yesterday. We did it in that cage, got out fast and watched results from this side of the bars."

"And what happened?"

"It behaved normally at first, licked the spot where we'd inserted the needle, wandered aimlessly around and threw us those looks of bewildered reproof which some dogs give when they think they've been kicked for nothing. After four minutes it collapsed, had a violent fit during which its body jerked spasmodically, it foamed at the mouth and gave muffled yelps."

"After that?"

"It recovered with surprising swiftness," Leeming detailed. "It went ten times around the cage, examining every part of it, and obviously seeking a means of escape. Finding none, it snarled at Balir, who happened to be standing nearest. It gave a display of ferocious hatred that had to be seen to be believed. Dill-water or not, it certainly wasn't the same dog as before."

"It seems mild enough now," Harper pointed out.

"I know. And that is highly significant, I believe. It raged against Balir. Then it turned its fury upon me. For a couple of hours it gave a display of maniac enmity toward anyone and everyone who came in sight. The emotional reaction to entrapment, see?"

"Could be."

"But after those couple of hours it changed character with the swift dexterity of an actor changing costumes between acts. The hatred vanished. The dog did its darnedest to ingratiate itself with Balir and put on so good a performance that he began to pity it. Knowing or sensing the effect, it redoubled its efforts to gain his friendship. However, Balir is a scientist. He refused to let himself be influenced by irrational sentiment. Therefore he did not respond."

"What did it do next?"

"It transferred its cajolings to me. I'll admit without shame that I had moments of feeling sorry for it—until I remembered that my sympathy could be expressed in only two ways, namely, to get within reach and fondle it, which might be most dangerous, or to release it, which could well be downright disastrous. So I remained hard."

"Is that all?"

"No. Early this morning it tried all its best tricks on Jim Calthorpe, who tends to its feeding. Calthorpe had been warned to use the slide-gate and keep out of the dog's reach no matter what. He refused to respond to its overtures. Now it is picking on you in your turn." Leeming glanced at the other and asked, "What do you deduce from such behaviour?"

"Constructive thought," Harper replied. "It has satisfied itself that escape is impossible without help. Its only chance is to find a weakling who'll cooperate. So it is testing the various candidates in order of arrival."

"That's what I suspect. But if we are correct, if it is being purposefully selective in its appeals, isn't that just a bit too clever for the average dog?"

"I don't know. I really don't know. As I told you before, I am no expert on canines. All I do know is that some dogs are alleged to be mighty smart and quite capable of coping with moderately complicated problems. Almost human is the conventional description for them."

"Yes, but the exceptionally intelligent dog has developed its mental status almost from birth. It hasn't acquired it all of a sudden, like being fitted with a new collar."

"Well?"

"This particular animal was as average a specimen as you could find in a long day's march. Now it's better than average. It has jumped from Dog I.Q. 70 to Dog I.Q. 100

or more. That is somewhat alarming in view of the circumstances. It points to a conclusion we hoped you could confirm. We are going to have a difficult time proving it without your help."

"There's a satisfactory way out," Harper suggested, "if anyone has the guts to take it."

"And what may that be?"

"Knock off that hound, recover the hell-juice from it, resquirt it into a human being. Or if you can spare the stuff you showed me in the lab, use that and save yourself time and trouble."

"Impossible!" declared Leeming.

"Show me an injected human being and I can tell you positively whether or not you have tracked down and isolated the real cause of all the trouble."

"Unthinkable!" Leeming said.

"Don't talk silly," Harper reproved. "How can it be unthinkable, seeing that I've thought of it?"

"You know what I mean. We cannot subject a fellow being to such a drastic test."

"It's a bit late for science to start taking count of moral considerations. The time for that was fifty years ago. Today, one more dirty trick will pass unnoticed. The public has got used to the idea that we've all degenerated to a bunch of guinea-pigs."

Leeming let that pass with no more than a disapproving frown, then said, "It might be all right if we could get a volunteer. Where are we going to find one? Would *you* offer your body for this?"

"I would not. And even if I were daft enough to submit, I would not be permitted to do so. Uncle Sam thinks me too precious to lose." He tapped Leeming's chest with a heavy forefinger. "And that fact alone suggests where you may get your experimental carcase, namely, from among those who aren't precious, those whose loss won't matter a hoot to anyone, even to themselves."

"What do you mean?"

"There are thugs in the death-house waiting to be hung, electrocuted or gassed. Offer any of them the one-in-a-thousand chance to gain release and watch him jump at it. Tell him that you want him to take a squirt. If he goes under, well, he's facing that as it is. But if you can cure him he'll be given a pardon and freed. Maybe Old Whiskers will find him a government job as a reward for public service."

"I have no authority to make such an extra-judicial bargain."

"Somebody has. Find him and keep kicking his pants until he wakes up."

"I doubt whether anyone less than the President could do it and even he'd have to stretch his powers to the limit."

"All right. Then chivvy the President. If you don't go after him somebody else will—and for a more formidable purpose."

"Look, Wade, talk comes cheap. Performance is a different matter altogether. Have you ever tried moving the top brass?"

"Yes."

"How far did you get?" Leeming asked with interest.

"I reached General Conway and got him on the hop good and proper. Come to think of it, he's the boy to ask for a hunk of forked meat. Tell him exactly what's happened here, what I've said to you, what you want to do about it. Tell him your test-subject has got to be a man and nothing less than a man. Dump the problem right in his lap and tell him that so far as you're concerned he's stuck with it. He won't nurse it any longer than he can help, you can bet on that!"

Harper studied the dog again while letting Leeming think it over. The Labrador whined, made pawing motions between the bars. It looked every inch a dog and nothing else save a dog. But that was no proof for or against. Elsewhere slunk creatures who bore equally close resemblance to people but were not people. The number one question: was this animal still a mere dog or had it become in effect a weredog?

He tried to listen to its mind as it begged his attention, and he heard precisely nothing. A blank, a complete blank. His natural range of reception just wasn't wide enough to pick up emanations from other than his own species. He switched from listening and probed at it sharply, fiercely, in manner that had brought immediate reaction from hiders in human shape. It had no effect upon the dog, which continued its fawning with obvious unconsciousness of his mental stabbing.

The silent experiment served only to confirm what he had already known: that the canine brain functions solely with respect to its own kind and that the so-called ability of dogs to read thoughts is no more than an expert appraisal of gestures, expressions, mannerisms and vocal tones. Because of that the Labrador represented a sterile line of research upon which Leeming had entered in good faith but little chance of satisfactory conclusion. Having got this far, it could be taken no farther. Another and more progressive line must involve a higher form of life.

Leeming broke into his meditation by saying, "I don't like it and I don't think I'll get away with it. Nevertheless I am willing to bait Conway providing you're standing by to back me up. He might listen to you when he won't to me."

"You don't know until you've tried."

"I do know that I am a scientist while he is a military figurehead. We don't talk the same language. The academic voice reasons while the voice of authority barks. If he can't or won't understand what I'm trying to explain and needs some cussing to make head or tail of it, you take the phone and use the necessary swear-words."

"Conway isn't that dopey," Harper answered. "High rank doesn't create a hollowhead despite certain exceptions that prove the rule."

"Let's go to my office," suggested Leeming. "You get hold of him then I'll see what can be done."

Harper called Jameson first, said, "I'm at the Biological Research Laboratories as probably you are aware, you having had something to do with bringing me here. I'm going to put through a call to General Conway. Doctor Leeming wants a brief talk with him."

"Then why get on to me?" Jameson asked.

"Because I've tried to reach Conway before, remember? It's like seeking to hold the hand of God. And neither Leeming nor I have the time or patience to be messed around by every underling in Washington. It's up to you to tell them to shove my call straight through."

"See here, Harper——"

"Shut up!" Harper ordered. "You've used me plenty. Now I'm using you. Get busy and do as you're told."

He slammed the instrument on to its rack, sat in a handy chair, scowled at the phone and snorted.

Leeming said apprehensively, "Who is this Jameson?"

"A big cheese in the F.B.I."

"And *you* tell *him* where *he* gets off?"

"It's the first time," said Harper. "And from what I know of him it'll also be the last." He brooded a bit, darkened in colour and snapped, "Anyway, why should one bunch of guys do all the order-giving and another all the order taking? Time we reversed roles once in a while, isn't it? Is this a democracy or am I deluded?"

"Now, now," protested Leeming. "Don't pick on me. I just accept things as they are."

"Like hell you do. If some of you scientists had been more content to leave well alone we'd all——" He let the rest go unsaid, chewed his bottom lip a piece, finished, "Take no notice. Once a month I have to give forth or go bang. Jameson's had long enough to ensure some action. If he hasn't taken steps by now he doesn't intend to."

"My bet is that he's done nothing."

"The odds are greatly in your favour, much as I hate to admit it." Harper regained the phone. "Anyway, we'll see."

His call went through, a youthful face appeared in his instrument's visiscreen.

"My name is Wade Harper," he told the face. "I want to speak to General Conway and it's urgent."

"Just a moment, please." The face went away, was replaced by another, older, more officious.

"About what do you wish to talk to the General?" inquired the newcomer.

"What's it to do with you?" demanded Harper toughly. "Go straight to Connie and find out once and for all whether or not he will condescend to have a word with me."

"I'm afraid I cannot do that unless I can first brief him on the subject matter of your——" The face ceased talking, glanced sidewise, said hurriedly, "Pardon me a moment," and disappeared. A few seconds later it returned wearing a startled expression. "Hold on, Mr. Harper. We're switching you through as speedily as possible."

Harper grinned at the now empty screen and said to Leeming, "Looks like you've lost your bet. Jameson got into motion although a bit slow at it."

"That surprises me."

"It surprises me, too. And it goes to show something or other if I had time to think it out."

The visiscreen registered eccentric patterns as the line was switched through intercom-boards, then cleared and held General Conway's austere features.

"What is it, Mr. Harper?"

Giving a short, succinct explanation, Harper handed the phone to Leeming who detailed the current state of affairs, ended by expressing his need for a human subject and the hope that Conway could do something about it.

"I disapprove such a tactic," declared Conway flatly.

Leeming reddened and said, "In that case, General, we can make no more progress. We are balked."

163

"Nonsense, man! I appreciate your desire and the inge-
nuity of what you suggest. But I cannot spend valuable
hours seeking some legal means of making use of a con-
demned felon when such a move is superfluous and unnec-
essary."

"I make the request only because I deem it necessary,"
Leeming pointed out.

"You are wrong. You have been sent four bodies of known
victims. Two more have become available today and you
will receive them shortly. With the spread of this peril and
the increase in number of people affected it becomes inevitable that before long we shall succeed in capturing one
alive. What more could you want than that?"

Leeming sighed and persisted patiently, "A live victim
would help but not conclusively. The most incontrovertible
proof of a cause is a demonstration that it creates the characteristic effect. I cannot demonstrate contagion with the
aid of a subject already riddled with it."

"Perhaps not," agreed Conway. "But such a subject, being
more communicative than a dog, can be compelled to identify the cause himself. It should not be beyond your wit to
devise a suitable technique for enforcing what might be
termed self-betrayal."

"Offhand I can think of only one way to achieve that,"
Leeming said. "And the trouble with it is that it's likely to
be long and tedious and it will mean considerable working
in the dark."

"What method?"

"Assuming that this virus is the true cause—which is
still a matter of doubt—we must seek an effective antigen.
Our proof will then rest upon our ability to cure the live
specimen. If we fail——"

"A cure has *got* to be found," asserted Conway, in manner
making it final and beyond all dispute. "Somehow, anyhow.
The only alternative is longterm, systematic extermination
of all victims on an eventual scale that none dare contem-

164

plate. Indeed, we could well be faced by a majority problem far too large for a minority to overcome, in which case the minority is doomed and humanity along with it."

"And you think that the life of one hardened criminal is too high a price to pay for freedom from that fate?" asked Leeming shrewdly.

"I think nothing of the sort," Conway contradicted. "I would unhesitatingly sacrifice the entire population of our prisons had I the power to do so and were I convinced that it was our only hope. But I have not the power and I am not convinced of the necessity."

"Let me speak to him," urged Harper, seeing Leeming's look of despair. He got the phone, gazed belligerently at the face in the screen knowing that it was now looking at his own. "General Conway, you say you lack the power and you're not persuaded?"

"That is correct," Conway agreed.

"The President, if consulted, might think differently. He has the necessary authority or, if not, can obtain it. Aren't you usurping his right to make a decision about this?"

"Usurping?" Conway repeated the word as if it were the ultimate in insults. He gathered himself together with visible effort, spoke in tones of restraint, "The President cannot work more than twenty-four hours per day. Therefore he deputes certain of his powers and responsibilities. I am now exercising some of the authority so assigned."

"By virtue of which you have his ear while others have not," Harper riposted. "So how about putting the matter to him?"

"No."

"All right. I am no longer asking you to do so. I am telling you to do so."

"Telling me?" The other registered incredulity.

"That's what I said: I am telling you. Refusal to co-operate is a game at which two can play. You can take

165

Leeming's proposition to the President or count me out of this fracas as from now."

"You cannot do that."

"I can."

"You know full well that we're dependent upon you to make positive identification where opportunity arises. You cannot possibly stand idly by knowing what's happening, watching it happen and doing nothing."

"I can. And what's more, I shall. You aren't the only one who can make like a mule."

"This is outrageous!" General Conway exploded.

"It's mutinous, too," endorsed Harper, showing indecent relish. "It's barefaced treachery. You could have me shot for it. Try it and see what good it does you. I'd be even less useful dead than dumb."

Conway breathed heavily while his face showed exasperation, then he said, "Against my better judgment I will take this up with the President and do my best to persuade him. I promise to try get the required action with minimum of delay but I offer no guarantee of success."

"Your word is plenty good enough for me," said Harper. "You're an officer and a gentleman. And in our antagonistic ways we're both working for the same end, aren't we?"

He got a grunt of irritation for that, put down the phone, eyed Leeming. "He'll do it. He's the sort who sticks to a promise like grim death once it's been forced out of him."

"You've got a nerve," offered Leeming, showing a touch of envy. "You've got so much nerve I wonder you've any friends. Someday you'll push it too far and somebody will slap your skull into its underlying mess."

"What are you talking about? Conway's a man and I'm a man. We both get haircuts, both wear pants. Once upon a time we both bawled and had our diapers changed. And we'll both smell as bad a month after we're dead. Am I supposed to kiss his feet in between times?"

"No, I suppose not."

"Then we're in sweet agreement." He consulted his wrist-watch. "Before I go there's one thing I'd like to know, if you can tell me."

"What's that?"

"How does this progressive disease become epidemic? How is it passed from one to another?"

"The same way as the dog got it," Leeming informed. "That girl Joyce Whittingham had received an injection in the upper arm, presumably with the blood of a victim."

"We can't say for certain that the dog has got it."

"No, but we do know the Whittingham girl had it. And we know she'd received an injection. So had two others. The fourth corpse had a plaster-covered cut that told the same story. My guess is that their reactions were the same as the dog's, a few minutes' confusion, collapse into a brief fit, rapid recovery."

"Well, the fact that contact alone evidently is not suffi-cient helps a little," mused Harper. "It means a prospect can't be taken just by sneezing in his direction. He has to be grabbed and held long enough to receive and get over a shot, eh?"

Leeming nodded and went on, "If this virus is not the actual cause it's a definite by-product, and if it's not the cause, well"—he spread hands expressively—"we're at a complete loss for any other."

"Anything else you can tell me about it?"

"Yes. It locates itself in the brain and spinal column. That is its natural habitat. The rest is theory and you can have it for what it's worth. I believe that the virus increases until it overflows into the bloodstream and thereby creates an urge to transmit the surplus, to seek another circulatory system leading to another brain and spinal column. You can think of it as the non-human equivalent of sexual desire, the actual transference being a substitute for copulation. It's

167

the irresistible response to the universal law: be fruitful and multiply."

"Humph!" Harper stewed that a while. He was curious about how transmission from creature to creature was accomplished on the world of origin. Did the preferred hosts on Venus take the shape of a lifeform high enough to manufacture and manipulate hypodermic needles? Or were they something lower in the scale of life, something peculiarly fanged and able to transmit impregnated blood with a single bite?

He suspected the latter. No matter how alien from the terrestrial viewpoint, this plague was born of Nature, designed to exist in masterful symbiosis with a similarly evolved partner. Therefore the mode of increase was likely to be natural rather than artificial and the injection-technique used on Earth was nothing but a substitute justified by proving satisfactory.

If all these bald assumptions happened to be correct, that imprisoned dog might well be capable of creating its own rescuer and much-wanted ally by getting in one good snap at an unwary leg or by licking a hand on which was a minute cut. The presence of virus in its saliva could open the gates to freedom and a wholesale conversion of human forms. Theoretically the animal was more dangerous than a cobalt bomb.

"If you want my advice," he said to Leeming, "you'd do well to put an end to that dog before it puts an end to you."

"Don't worry. We're used to coping with such matters here. Nobody goes near enough to be spat upon, much less touched."

"You know your own business. And it's high time I resumed tending to mine. I am going home, back to the trap that Conway hopes will catch a live one." Harper let go a harsh chuckle. "If I'm dead out of luck they may bring you a struggling zombie that will prove to be me."

"What d'you mean?" inquired Leeming, wide-eyed.

"Never mind. Let's find the escort. If I return without them there'll be the deuce to pay." He glanced at the ceiling as if appealing to heaven. "What a world!"

Chapter 11

Rausch was hanging around the office when Harper arrived in the morning. He said, "We stayed put until eight last evening thinking you'd be sure to return here. If your guard hadn't advised us that they'd delivered you safely home we'd have been stuck in this dump all night."

"What with one thing and other, including three stops *en route*, I got back too late." Hanging his hat, Harper sat at his desk, reached for the mail. "Where's Norris? How come you're here? I thought you were making an ambush of the Baum place?"

"We've abandoned hope of catching anyone there. The news about the Baums appeared in yesterday's last editions and got reported as an automobile smash. A pic on the wrecked car being towed away was shown in the pane's midnight summary. Despite the cover-up it's more than enough to warn off the Baums' playmates. We'll grab nobody there if we try for a year."

"Well, all I can say is that some people appear pretty

good at thwarting the Feds." Harper tore open a couple of envelopes, rapidly scanned their contents. "They're much too sharp for my liking. And they're playing hob with my pet theory that basically all criminals are dopes." Then he glanced up from a letter, added thoughtfully, "If this bunch can properly be called criminals."

"How else can you describe them?"

"As a menace. A red-hot menace. Like a gang of dogs with rabies. Or a group of smallpox carriers hiding from the health authorities. But worse than that, infinitely worse." He re-read the letter, dumped it into a wire basket. "Where did you say Norris has gone?"

"I didn't say. If it's any satisfaction to you he has dashed out on what is probably another fruitless trip."

"What do you mean by 'another'?"

"Yesterday, while you were absent," explained Rausch, "the boys picked up no less that eight alleged McDonalds. It would have been a top notch performance if any of them had turned out to be McDonald. But none were. Half an hour ago Norris rushed away for a look at number nine."

"How's he checking?"

"Easily enough. He has mug-shots, prints and so forth. He's got sufficient to pin down the right one beyond all shadow of doubt. We've not yet laid hands on the right one."

"I'd give much to know how he's keeping out of reach," Harper observed. "The technique might be extremely useful to me some day."

Rausch stared at him. "What's on your mind?"

"Embezzlement." Then he gave a false laugh. "But of course. How silly of me. If I abscond with this outfit's money I'm merely taking my own. Which proves yet again that an employer can do no wrong. Think it over."

"I am thinking," informed Rausch suspiciously. "And I think you're kidding me. I also think it isn't funny."

"It wasn't intended to be." He grabbed more mail, ripped

off the covers. "Anything else happened that I ought to know about?"

"Your police friend Riley called in the afternoon, became nosey about where you'd gone."

"Did you tell him?"

"How could we? We didn't know ourselves. And even if we'd possessed the information we wouldn't have given it. He is not entitled to be told."

"Did he state the purpose of his visit?"

"No. I got the impression that it was just a casual drop-in for a gab. He said he'd call again today. He fooled around trying to make your secretary then went."

Harper dropped the letter he was holding, eyed Rausch sharply. "Say that again, the bit about my secretary."

"Riley horsed about with her a bit then departed."

"Never! Never in a month of Sundays! He wouldn't make a pass at Moira if she begged him to eat her. That's why I kid him about it. He's so solidly married that it's boring."

"He did," asserted Rausch. "Maybe the solidity is becoming slightly undermined. You wouldn't know about that. You don't sleep with him."

Harper relaxed, said, "You've made a point there. Moira is due to arrive in about ten minutes. I'll ask her about this."

"I don't see the need. Not unless you've a lien on her love-life."

"The bond between us is firmly based upon a mutual affection for hard cash," Harper informed. "That and no more."

"Have it your own way," said Rausch, shrugging. He mooched into the workshop, amused himself watching micromanipulators being assembled, came back when Moira appeared.

Waiting until she had settled herself behind her typewriter, Harper asked, "What is this about you and Riley?"

She was taken aback. "I don't understand, Mr. Harper."

"I'm told the lumbering elephant made a play for you."

"Oh no, not really." She gained a slight flush. "He only joshed me a bit. I knew he meant nothing by it."

"But he's never done that before, has he?"

"No, Mr. Harper. I think he was just filling in time, not finding you here."

Harper leaned forward, gazing at her but not picking her mind. "Did he try to date you?"

She was shocked and a little indignant. "Certainly not. He did offer me a theatre ticket someone had given him. He said he wasn't able to use it and I could have it."

"Did you accept it?"

"No. It was for last night. I had a date already and couldn't go."

"Was he disappointed when you refused the ticket?"

"Not that I noticed." Her attention shifted to the listening Rausch then back to Harper, her features expressing bafflement. "What is all this, anyway?"

"Nothing much, Lanky. I am trying to determine whether Riley was drunk or sober yesterday afternoon. It's an interesting speculation because never in my life have I known him to get stinko."

"A person doesn't have to be drunk to notice my existence," she gave back more than pointedly.

"That's the baby!" approved Rausch, coming in on her side. "You landed that one right on the button."

"Keep your beak out of my domestic affairs," ordered Harper. He picked up a letter. "Forget it, Moira. Let's get down to business. Take this reply to the Vester Clinic. Replacement titanium-alloy needles for Model Fourteen are immediately available in sets of six. We quote you——"

He had finished dictating and was presiding in the workshop when Norris returned sour-faced and said, "You wouldn't think so many people could have a superficial but passable resemblance to one wanted man."

"Meaning they'd grabbed another dud?"

"Yes. A paint-drummer sufficiently like McDonald to

173

make the pinch excusable. Moreover, he was in a devil of a hurry, lost his temper, tried to crash a road-block. That was his undoing."

"Look," said Harper, "McDonald escaped loaded with luggage and had at least an hour's start. Do you really suppose that he is still in this town?"

"No, I don't. I reckon the chances are a hundred to one against it. Not only have we found no trace of him but none of the Reeds or their car either. I think they slipped through the cordon and are now way out in the wilds. But we're passing up no chances no matter how remote."

"All right. Then I'll tell you something: if those three have escaped they've left at least one contact here."

"How do you know that?" Norris demanded.

"Because we whizzed past one yesterday. I tried to get the cavalcade to go after him but they refused to stop. They had their orders and they stuck to them. It shows how blind obedience can make a hash of initiative."

Norris did not like that last remark but let it go by and inquired, "Did you get any clue to his identity?"

"Not a one. If I had I'd have told you last night and saved your time. He might be anybody, anybody at all. The best I can do is guess."

"Go ahead and do some guessing. You've made a few lucky shots so far."

"This is a wild one fired entirely at random," Harper told him, almost apologetically. "I can't get rid of the idea that about the safest place in the world for a hunted man is a town where every man jack is hunting for some other character. He benefits from the general distraction, see? His safety factor is increased more than somewhat by virtue of the obvious fact that you can concentrate on one thing only by ignoring other things."

"Go on," urged Norris, interested.

"So if the presence of my carcase makes this town an

area of irresistible attraction to the opposition, and everyone here is chasing around in search of McDonald——"

"Finish it, man, finish it!"

"What a wonderful set-up for William Gould." Harper regarded the other levelly. "Who's looking for *him*?"

"The entire country. You know that."

"I'm not considering the entire country. I'm thinking only of this town. Unlike the rest of the country, it's obsessed by McDonald to such an extent that Gould could step in and baby-sit for you and you'd pay him two dollars with thanks." He drummed restless fingers on the desk while that sank in, then added for good measure, "After which it would never be the same baby again."

Rausch chipped in, "Whether that guess is on or off the mark makes no difference. Gould is wanted as badly as McDonald. It would do no harm to distribute a local reminder of that fact."

"It wouldn't at that," agreed Norris. "You go out and see to it right now." Norris watched Rausch hurry out then returned attention to Harper. "Where do you dig up these notions?"

"The onlooker sees the most of the game. And as I told you before, I've been on the run myself while you have not. It helps a lot when one tries to put oneself in the other fellow's shoes. That's why the first and perhaps one of the best detectives in history was an ex-con with a long record."

"Who was that?"

"Eugene Françoise Vidocq."

"I'll look him up some day," Norris promised. "If by then I'm not in the jug busily completing my education."

"You'll never look him up. He died long before you were born. All the same, I——"

He shut up as his mental searchlight made one of its periodic circlings and found something in the surrounding ocean of emanations. He was quiet while his mind listened.

It was coming again.

Gobble-gobble.

Failing to notice this sudden preoccupation, Norris prompted, "You were about to say?"

"Nothing of consequence. Let it pass."

Harper made a disparaging gesture, returned to his office and sat erect in his chair. He felt under one arm to make sure the gun was readily available.

"Moira," he said quietly, "there's a packet for Schultz-Masters ready in the shop. It's urgent. I'd like you to take it to the post office at once. See that it goes by the midday mail. You need not hurry back. It'll do if you return after lunch."

"What about this correspondence, Mr. Harper?"

"You'll have all afternoon to cope with it. Put a move on and get rid of that consignment so that I'll have an answer ready if Schultz-Masters start bawling over the phone."

"Very well." She adjusted her hat on her head, picked up her handbag, went into the workshop and collected the package.

Going to the window, he watched her hurrying along the street in the direction opposite to that from which danger was coming. Well, that got her away from the scene of prospective trouble.

A couple of burly characters walked ten yards behind her rapidly clicking heels. They knew where she was going because the mike planted in the office had informed Norris or whoever happened to be listening-in. But they weren't going to let her out of their sight and hadn't done from the start of fixing the trap. It was just as well.

He did not open the window as he had done at the approach of Ambrose Baum. Leaving it fastened, he stood behind it surveying as much of the street as could be seen while stretching his receptive power to the utmost.

This time he was not going to make the mistake of transmitting a mental stab and getting the foe to flee with the knowledge so ardently sought. He was going to do no more than listen and thus leave the other mind blissfully unconscious of its open state. True, that meant he dare not stimulate desired information and had to rest content with whatever the hidden thinker saw fit to offer, regardless of whether said offerings made sense or nonsense.

Leaving the window he flopped into his chair, stared unseeingly at Moira's desk while he listened and waited. It was a unique and most curious experience despite previous brief encounters.

Judging by the chronically slow increase in amplitude of the distant impulses the oncoming entity was progressing at little more than a crawl; probably walking warily with frequent pauses for pretended examinations of shop windows. It was not hesitant in the manner of one fearful and on edge. On the contrary, it was cold-bloodedly aware of many dangers and trying to side-step any that became apparent.

The mind did not identify itself in human terms because at the moment it was not thinking in human terms. Cogitatively, it was bilingual. The queer ganderlike gobble-gobble was another-world sound track synchronised with another-world thought-forms. It was obedient to a habit born of countless centuries of possession by doing its thinking in the mental terms of its faraway hosts. Occupation of a completely human-type brain in no way handicapped this function. All brains utilize the data filed therein and this one was armed with knowledge of two worlds and at least two distinct species.

Even though directing his attention elsewhere, Harper was able to do some thinking of his own. What if this gradually nearing sneaker were none other than William

Gould? How could he hope to walk in on Harper and get away with whatever he schemed to do?

It was hardly likely that his purpose was to kill, even at cost of his own life, because the foe would gain little enough from that. The prize they wanted and must secure at all costs was accurate knowledge of the means by which they could be identified. To slay the only one able to reveal this secret would leave them as perilously ignorant as before.

Their sole rational tactic was to capture and hold Harper for long enough to force the truth out of him. Once successfully grabbed, the technique of compulsion would be simple and effective. They'd take possession of him exactly as others had become possessed, after which they would find the wanted datum recorded in his mind, and it would be theirs, entirely theirs to use as they wished.

Nothing less than that would tell them what they had to combat and enable them to devise means of mastering any similar threats from any other source. Therefore the oncomer must be at least a scout tentatively tasting local defences or at most a would-be kidnapper hoping to pull the job single-handed somehow, heaven alone knew how.

In the latter event there must be more to the present situation than was yet evident to the eyes. The enemy was far from stupid. No delegate of theirs would try to snatch Harper in these circumstances unless playing a part that offered at least a moderate chance of success.

The alien thought-stream had grown much stronger now and was replete with brief, unrecognizable scenes like glimpses of some nightmarish landscape. Harper removed attention from it for a moment while he scoured the area for minds like it. Perhaps there were a dozen or twenty converging by prearrangement upon his address, hoping to take him by sheer weight of numbers.

There were not. He failed to detect any others. Only this one was approaching and if any more of them were around they must be lurking beyond detectable range. If so, had they chosen their concealing distance by pure accident or had they started to make some very shrewd guesses?

Still he did not probe. Neither did he warn Norris as he was supposed to do. He sat tight, determined for the time being to play things his own way. Regulation tactics had gained nothing but several corpses and a picture of a fuzzy ball. A little irregularity might prove more profitable. He did not bother to consider the risk involved or the possible cost to his own skin. His lack in this respect was more the measure of his impatience than his courage.

The other mind was now passing beneath his window but he did not try to take a look that, if noticed, might create premature alarm. If it continued onward along the sidewalk, ignoring his front door, he was going to get out fast and nail it. But if it came in he was going to sit right there and meet it as man to mock-man.

It turned in at the front door and immediately the thought-stream switched to human terms with all the brilliant clarity of the pane when it is suddenly adjusted after being mistily off-focus. There was a reason for that. The arrival had come into contact with a couple of agents on guard and immediately adapted itself to cope with a human situation. It was done with speed and polished perfection possible only to a lifeform that had never worn anything but fleshy masks because it had no face of its own.

And in that pregnant moment Harper learned whom to expect. He read it in the minds of the agents even as they swapped a few words with the newcomer.

"Is the orang-outang here? Or has he gone out chasing a percentage?"

"He's warming his office chair."

"Mind if I bust in?"

"Go help yourself."

Harper smiled grimly. He picked up the agents' mental images as they let the enemy walk through. He changed attention to Norris, outside sitting on a bench in the workshop, almost saw through his eyes as idly he watched the other reach the door.

Then the gobbler entered and Harper said in the manner of one completely fooled, "Hello, Riley. What brings you here?"

Helping himself to the absent Moira's chair, Riley seated himself carefully, looking at Harper and all unwittingly gave him a piece of his mind.

"He is supposed to know us on sight in some mysterious way. Everything adds up to that fact. But he does not react in this case. That is strange. Something's wrong somewhere."

Vocally, Riley responded, "I'm keeping my finger on your pulse."

"Why?"

"There's a five thousand dollar reward in the bag for whoever finds Alderson's killer. Captain Ledsom hasn't forgotten it despite all the hullabaloo about three fellows who've done nobody knows what. I haven't forgotten it either. It's a lot of money."

"So you're hoping to sell me for that sum eventually?"

"No, I'm not. I don't believe you did it. But I think you know more than you've told. And I'm betting that when all this ruckus is over you'll get busy on it."

"And then?"

"You may need my help. Or I may need yours. Between the two of us we might lay hands on that sack of gold."

"You're becoming mercenary in your old age, and sloppy to boot."

"What do you mean, sloppy?"

Carefully steering the conversation into mentally revealing channels, Harper said, "Fooling with Moira while I'm away."

"Bunk!"

"Cajoling her with a theatre ticket."

That did it.

The responding flash of secret thought lasted no more than two or three seconds but was detailed enough to present the picture. Moira innocently enjoying the show in seat U.17. William Gould apparently doing likewise in U.18. Conversation between acts, a planned pick-up and stroll home—with Moira finishing up no longer human.

Gould was young, attractive, had enough glamour to make the plot workable. Only a previous date had spoiled it. In any case, Moira's unshakable escort would have proved troublesome unless Gould escaped them by persuading her to invite him into her home. Perhaps that was what he had planned. The brief stream from Riley's brain lacked data on this point.

"I couldn't use it," said Riley. "What should I have done with it? Masticate it?"

"You could have given it to your wife."

Another picture came in response to that and confirmed what Harper had reluctantly taken for granted. Riley's wife was no longer a wife. She was a living colony of fuzzy balls that had the urge to spread but were utterly indifferent to the sex of the host. By implication, that added one more datum to knowledge of the foe, namely, that a person could not be confiscated by means of sexual union with one of the possessed. The virus could not or preferred not to penetrate by osmosis; it needed direct entry from the suffused bloodstream to the new bloodsteam.

"She doesn't like to go by herself," said Riley. "What are you griping about, anyway? Why should you care where Moira goes or what she does of an evening?"

And then, *"There's something significant in this sudden concern for Moira. It smacks of deep suspicion. I don't see how he can be suspicious. Either he actually knows or he doesn't, and by the looks of it he does not know."*

"According to the Feds I'm in some sort of danger," informed Harper. "If so, Moira shares it simply by working with me and being closest to me. I don't want her to suffer for my sake."

That had its calculated effect by lulling the other mind. It was much like playing a conversational version of chess, Harper thought. Move and countermove, deceitfulness and entrapment, prompt seizure of any advantage or opening likely to lead toward checkmate.

The next moment Riley emphasized the simile by making a dangerous move. "That may be so. But I am not Gould, McDonald or Langley. So why pick on me?"

There was nothing for it but to accept the challenge by making a bold advance.

Eyeing him steadily, Harper said, "I am not yawping about you personally. I am uneasy because I don't know who gave you that ticket."

The mental answer came at once: Gould.

"What does it matter?" Riley evaded. "How was he to know I wouldn't use it myself or that I'd offer it to Moira?"

"Oh, let's drop the subject," Harper suggested, with pretended weariness. "This chase after three men has got me jumpy enough to question the motives of my own mother."

Soothing lotion again. The opposing brain mopped it up solely because it was plausible.

"The sooner they're picked up the better I'll like it," continued Harper, offering fresh bait. "Take McDonald, for instance. He was around these parts quite recently. A smart copper like you ought to be able to find him."

Eureka! Out came the reaction as clearly as if written upon paper. Gould, McDonald, the Reeds and two others previously unknown were clustered together in Riley's own house, waiting, waiting for Harper to come along on the strength of whatever pretext Riley could think up.

So here was the real purpose of the visit. Riley had not yet got around to the enticement but would do so before leaving. Come into my parlour, said the spider to the fly.

And in due course—it was hoped—Harper would drop

in upon the Rileys while his bunch of shadows politely hung around outside. He would go in like a lamb to the slaughter and, after a while, emerge visibly no different. The shadowers would then escort him home and leave him to weird dreams of a far-off land where blind bugs serviced themselves from portions of their own dead and poison-spiked cacti tottered around on writhing roots and few agile creatures had souls to call their own.

The foreign intelligence now animating Riley proved itself sharp enough to bait the baiter. "What makes you think that I should succeed where a regiment of agents has failed?"

Harper had to react fast to that one. "Only because you're a local boy. They're out-of-towners. You've sources of information not available to them. You know the ropes, or ought to after all these years."

It was not quite enough to halt the probe.

"Then why didn't they rely on the police instead of pushing themselves in by the dozens?"

"Ask me another," Harper said, shrugging. "Probably someone's decided that the more men on the job, the better."

"It has bought them nothing so far, has it?" asked Riley, seemingly a little sarcastic.

But it was not sarcasm. It was temptation hidden under a cloak of mild acidity. It was an invitation to make mention of the Baums, to come out with a reply indicating how they'd been recognized for what they were.

The mind of Riley was working fast, driven on by the urgency of the slime that commanded it. But seek as he might, he could not find a satisfactory explanation of the contrast between his own immunity and the speedy downfall of others of his type.

Temporarily, the only theory that fitted the circumstances was an unsatisfactory one, namely, that Harper's menacing ability functioned haphazardly or under certain specific conditions not present at this moment. However, no theory served to explain how it was done. On the contrary, the existing situation complicated the puzzle. What could be the nature of positive detection that operated only in spasms?

In the few seconds that Riley spent mulling these problems, Harper strove to cope satisfactorily with some of his own. By dexterous use of leading comments how much could he get out of Riley without giving himself away? How best to frame questions and remarks that would draw essential information from the other's mind? How to find out the means by which Riley himself had been taken over, how many others had become possessed, their names, their hiding-places, their plans and so forth?

"No," agreed Harper, thwarting him. "It hasn't gained them a cent so far."

Refusing to be stalled, Riley took it further. "Except that they've wiped out a couple of boys named Baum. We got a routine report from a patrolman about that. It wasn't an auto accident, no matter what the official version says. It was the result of a fracas in which you were involved."

Harper offered no remark.

"Maybe it's no business of mine," Riley went on with just the right mixture of resentment and persuasiveness, "but if I knew how and why the Baums were finished it might give me a lead to this McDonald."

"Why?" asked Harper, looking straight at him. "Is there any connection?"

"You know there is. It's all part of the same crazy business."

"Who says so?"

The other's mind had a moment of confusion born of sudden need to cast doubt on what it knew to be true.

"Well, isn't it?"

"Maybe and maybe not," said Harper, keeping a perfectly expressionless face.

"Damn it, if you don't know what's going on, who does?"

That was another dexterously dug pitfall, a call to produce an evasive answer that might reveal plenty by its various implications.

Harper side-stepped the trap, feeling cold down his back as he did it.

"All I can tell you is that they were known to have become pally with McDonald. Therefore they were wanted for questioning. Immediately they were spotted they fled for dear life and one thing led to another." He paused, fought cunning with cunning by adding as a mystified afterthought, "It beats me completely. They weren't accused of a major crime, so why did they flee?"

Turmoil grew strong in the opposing brain. It had been asked the very question to which it desired the answer, as a matter of life or death. The assumed holder of the secret was seeking the solution himself.

Why did they flee?

Why did they flee?

Round and round whirled the problem and persistently threw out the only answer, namely, that the Baums had run because they'd become known and had realized *how* they'd become known. Therefore the mode of identification must be self-revealing. The possessed could not be fingered without sensing the touch.

Yet now that it was put to actual test there was no recognition, no dramatic exposure, no feelable contact, no touch, nothing.

What's the answer to that?

"As a guess, divide this world's bipeds into types A and B. The former is vulnerable because identifiable by some method yet to be discovered. Joyce Whittingham was of that type. So were the Baums. So might others be. But for unknown reasons type B is impervious to the power of Harper and any more who may share it. By sheer good fortune this body called Riley happens to be of that kind."

So the alien thought-stream ruminated while Harper listened, mentally thanking God that it had retained its pseudo-human role and not switched to transspatial double-talk.

It went on, *"If this notion should be correct, then salvation lies around the corner. We must learn the critical factor that protects type B and how to distinguish one type from another. Henceforth we must take over only type B. The vulnerable ones can be dealt with afterwards."*

We! The plural! Momentarily, in his concentration, Riley was thinking of himself as a mob!

Deep down inside himself Harper was sickened by this first-hand reminder of the ugly facts. The invader was a horde multi-millions strong. Each capture of a human body was victory for a complete army corps represented by a few drops of potent goo in which the individual warrior was—what?

A tiny sphere of hazy outline.

A fuzzy ball.

My brother's keeper!

Determined to make the most of his opportunity while it lasted, Harper went on, "Someone once remarked that the only difference between those in prison and those outside is that the latter have never been found out. Possibly the Baum brothers had something on their consciences and wrongly supposed it had been discovered. So they ran like jackrabbits."

"Could be," admitted Riley, while his thoughts said, *"It doesn't fit the facts. They had no cause for flight other than realization of betrayal. Harper knew them for what they were but refuses to admit it. That is at least consistent of him. He always did keep a tight mouth about his power."* A pause, followed by, *"Yet at the moment he lacks that power. Why? The reason must be found!"*

"Anyway, what's the use of gabbing?" Harper continued, craftily spurring the other on. "Talk gets us nowhere and I have work to do."

"You can't give me one useful hint concerning McDonald?"

"No. Go look for him yourself. You'll get plenty of kudos if you nail him. Besides, he may lead you to Gould, who is wanted just as badly."

"Gould?" He stared across, thinking, *"Do they know or suspect that he is in this town?"*

"And his contacts," added Harper, panning for paydirt. "Every one of them for the past three months."

The result was disappointing. He got fleeting, fragmentary pictures of a score of people without any means of determining who they were or where they lived, of what parts they were playing in this struggle for a world.

"When Gould and McDonald have been fastened down good and tight," he went on, "we may then have time to seek afresh for Alderson's killer and try for that five thousand you covet."

He was doing fine. The reference to Alderson brought the hoped-for reaction: a fragment of memory radiated with vividness. McDonald holding Joyce Whittingham while Gould sank a needle into her arm. Joyce struggling and screaming. A police cruiser suddenly halting right behind. Alderson jumping out and making for the Thunderbug. Langley pulling a gun and dropping him before he could intervene. So Langley had done it.

Hah! That brought up something else of considerable significance. The country's entire forces of law and order, Riley included, had been alerted to capture three men, not two. Yet Riley had shown no curiosity about Langley. He had asked about McDonald. He had accepted without question the reminder concerning Gould. Any normal individual would have brought up the subject of the third quarry— unless he knew that he was dead. Did Riley know that? If so, how had he learned it? How to find out?

Daringly, he rushed the issue. "As for Langley, nobody need worry about him any more."

Riley said nothing vocally but did utter a mental, *"Of course not. He's finished."*

"Who told you?" asked Harper.

"Told me what?"

"About Langley?"

"I don't know what you mean. Nobody has said anything to me concerning him."

"I've just mentioned that Langley is out of the running," Harper reminded. "You made no remark, showed no surprise. So I took it for granted that it was old news to you though I can't imagine how you got hold of it."

"You're wrong," contradicted Riley, hastening to cover up a minor blunder. "It's the first I've heard of it. The information failed to sink in."

He was too late. His mind had lagged seconds behind Harper's wits and his tongue had come last in the field. Despite intervening hundreds of miles, Riley had known of Langley's end the moment it occurred. He had sensed it as surely as one may gaze across a valley at night and see a distant light become suddenly extinguished.

It was a wholly alien faculty having nothing in common with any human sense. The possessed enjoyed a peculiar awareness of the existence of their own kind, could follow it blindly until they had gravitated together. By the same token, loss of awareness with respect to one particular focal point meant death far away over the horizon. Just the bare fact of death, without any details.

The same sense could detect a dreadful urgency radiated by another, the equivalent of a cry for help. It was strictly non-telepathic. A psi-factor. In effect, Riley could look afar, see the life-light emanating from one of his own kind, see it winking a summons for assistance, see it go dark. No more than that.

Perhaps it was the ultimate form of what Earth called the herd instinct. An alien protective device evolved on another world where survival sometimes demanded a rapid gathering of the clans and the lone individual went under.

Therefore, elsewhere they must have a natural enemy, a constant antagonist not strong enough to keep them in total subjection, much less eliminate them, but sufficiently redoubtable to restrict their spread and help maintain a distant world's balance of competing life-forms.

What could it be? Some strong-stomached animal that craved and consumed a potent virus with all the avidity of a cat lapping cream? A creature capable of devouring a possessed body without harm to itself? Or something smaller which came like warrior ants in hordes of its own and lived by ingesting armies of the vicious?

The datum was precious enough to be worth discovering if it could be gotten. But how to get it? How could he entice it from a hostile and wary mind without giving himself away? How can one question a Venusian concerning the fauna and flora of Venus while successfully managing to uphold the pretence of regarding him as a natural born native of Earth?

Another expedition might pick up the information some day—providing it did not succumb to the same fate as the first. But if urgent problems were not solved here and now there would never be another expedition, or not one that was truly human.

Knowledge of a deadly enemy's own especial foe was there, right there across the desk, buried within a mastered brain. If only it could be extracted, the scientists could search Earth for a local counterpart fully as capable of handling this alien menace. It was a glittering prize worth far more in the long run than capture of all this world's afflicted. It meant ability to deal with the root cause instead of fooling around with the symptoms.

Harper sought frantically for a method of making a highly dangerous move appear disarmingly innocent. He looked into Riley's questioning eyes which all along had seemed entirely normal and gave no hint of what was lurking behind.

Wetting his lips, he said, "Langley and some other fellow were trapped. They shot it out like madmen. It proved impossible to take them alive."

Riley raised an eyebrow in false surprise. "Everybody knew he was wanted but nobody's been told what for. Judging by that reaction the reason must have been mighty serious. So where's the sense in all the secrecy?"

"Don't ask me. I have no say in government policy." He made a gesture of bafflement. "You know how the top boys sometimes love to be mysterious."

The other grunted in disdain.

Now then, this was it, the critical play. It had to be done delicately, like handling dynamite. One slip and there'd be an explosion of wild action with Norris and the others caught by surprise. Thank goodness Moira was out of it.

With a deceitfully reminiscent air, Harper went on, "It's possible that Langley really was cracked in the head. If so, I don't like it. Everyone has pet fears and I've got mine."

"Such as what?"

"When I was a small child I was afraid of big black dogs. Now I'm older I have a violent revulsion toward mental disease. I fear loonies." He pulled a face, nerved himself and made the move. "What scares *you* the most?"

By God, he got it! He got it as clearly and vividly as only a lifelong terror can be pictured. What's more, he felt sure that he recognized it, not by its form but by its brutal nature. And it was here, on Earth, waiting around and ready for use. He had to tighten his mouth to prevent himself from shouting aloud.

Standing up, Riley frowned at him and asked in taut tones, "What makes you ask me that?" And his mind followed on with, *"A while ago he said that talk was of no avail, that he was busy and had work to do. Yet he's been maintaining the conversation ever since. He has been*

190

prompting me repeatedly and I've had to keep avoiding his leads. Nevertheless he appears satisfied with answers that I've been careful not to give. How can that be?"

The enemy mentality was searching with swiftly mounting alarm. Telepathy was completely outside its experience, nothing like it having been encountered in its native habitat. But when an astute mind fails to solve a problem on the basis of recorded data and steps right outside of experience to seek a solution within the imagination, anything is possible.

At any moment Riley was going to conceive the formerly inconceivable.

Then would come the eruption.

Chapter 12

Casually scratching under one arm in order to have fingers near the gun, Harper said, "I don't know why I asked you. I'm not in the least interested. If you feel touchy on the subject you can attribute my question to mere yap. I've been doing too much of that considering the jobs waiting to be done. Go away and let me tend to my business."

He failed in his attempt to divert the thoughtstream into another direction.

"He has a weapon there," it flowed on. *"I have seen him carrying it many a time. He has his hand on it and cannot conceal his tenseness. He would not be like that if he knew nothing. Therefore he knows something in spite of all my attempts to hide it."* A puzzled pause, then, *"I came in the role of an old friend. Yet he makes ready to deal with me for what I am."*

Grinning at him, Harper withdrew the hand, used it to scratch his head instead. It was a mistake.

"By the Great Black Rock of Karsim, he can hear my thoughts!"

The desk went over with a crash that shook the floor as Harper dived headlong across it and grabbed the hand which Riley was digging into a pocket. Something small, oval and metallic lay in the pocket but did not come out.

Voicing a loud oath in no known language, Riley used his free hand to try to haul Harper from the pinioned one. He was a heavy, powerful man with a huge grip that had clamped itself unbreakably on many a struggling felon. Hauling with irresistible strength, he was caught unaware when Harper went willingly with the pull and helped it farther. The unexpected co-operation sent him teetering on his heels, at which point Harper shoved with all his might.

Together they fell to the floor, with Harper partly on top. Riley's eyes were aflame, his features crimson as he fought to beat off his opponent long enough to get at the object in his pocket. Pinning him down was like trying to fasten an enraged tiger to the earth.

A thick-knuckled fist landed squarely on Harper's mouth and brought a spurt of blood from split lips. The sight of it created a horrible eagerness in Riley's features. He redoubled his efforts to throw the other off, heaving tremendously and keeping his gaze on the blood.

Panting as he strove to maintain his position of vantage, Harper caught a knee-thrust in the stomach, whooshed expelled breath, spat crimson drops and hoarsed, "No you don't, you——!" He released his hold on Riley's right wrist, got a two-handed grip on his neck and dug thumbs into his windpipe.

At that point Norris jumped through the doorway, gun in hand, and bawled, "Break it up! Break it up, I tell you!"

Riley heaved with maniac force, tossed Harper off his middle, kicked at his head as he rolled aside and missed. He shot upright, glaring at Norris and showing complete disregard of the gun. He made a motion toward his pocket, came down flat before he could touch it as Harper twisted on the floor and snatched the feet from under him.

Clutching each other afresh, the two threshed around with bodies squirming and legs flailing right and left. A tall filing cabinet shuddered under their impact, rocked forward, toppled and flung a shower of business papers across the office. The telephone leaped from its rack, two bottles of ink and one of paste added themselves to the mess. The combatants continued to fight fiercely amid the litter.

Rausch and two more agents appeared just as Norris firmed his lips and stepped forward determined to end the battle. The four made a concerted rush that swept Harper aside and got Riley good and tight. They dragged him upright.

Sweating profusely, Riley stood in their grip, forced righteous indignation into his face and declaimed with plausible resentfulness, "The man's gone completely mad. He attacked me without warning and for no reason at all. There must be something wrong with him."

It was said with such a natural air that Norris had a nervy moment of wondering whether Harper had gone bad right under his nose and despite all their precautions.

"Feel in his pocket and see what he's got," suggested Harper. Sitting on the edge of the upended desk, he dabbed his bleeding lips with a handkerchief.

Norris did that, produced a grenade, examined it. "Army model, same as Baum used." He gazed hard-eyed at Riley. "Funny sort of thing for a police officer to carry around, isn't it?"

"He's not a police officer any more," Harper put in. "And he isn't Riley either. Rush him down to the Biological Research Laboratory. They need him there at once."

These words created a sudden frenzy in the prisoner. His arms were held but his legs were not. He kicked Norris in the middle, tore loose, tried to snatch the grenade. Norris bent forward doubled with agony, but held on to it. Riley pulled at him, gobbling and foaming, making strange whining noises and working his features almost out of recognition.

An agent sapped him. Riley rocked dazedly, let his hands hang. The agent slogged him again, a vicious crack devoid of mercy. Riley collapsed like an empty sack. He lay with eyes closed, lips shut and breathed with eerie bubbling sounds.

"I've no time for belly-kickers," said the agent.

Norris straightened himself painfully, his face white and strained. He held out the grenade. "Take it away some place where it can do no harm."

"Same applies to the owner," Harper reminded. "Tie him up so he can't choke himself with his own fingers and get him to the Bio. Lab."

"Is he——?"

"Yes, he is. And it's my fault. He had entry to this office and it's cost him his soul."

"I thought you were supposed to be able to smell them coming," Norris complained. "What's the use of us guarding you for half a mile around if they can walk in like this and——"

"I knew he was coming."

"Then why didn't you tell us? I was listening-in to your conversation and thought it decidedly fishy. You were needling him for some reason or other. But seeing that you had sounded no alarm we——"

"Look," said Harper firmly, "this is no time for explanations or post-mortems. Rush him to Doctor Leeming at the Bio. Lab. as fast as you can make it. And don't give him the slightest opportunity to finish himself on the way there. I'm giving you fair warning that if he can't escape he'll kill himself by any means to hand. He must be delivered alive and in one piece."

"All right."

Norris signed to the others. They lifted Riley, who now

had steel cuffs on wrists and ankles and was still unconscious. They carried him out.

Mopping his lips again, Harper stared moodily at the
wreckage of his office. He was not really seeing it, though.
He was physically and spiritually shaken and striving to
overcome it. Crazy circumstances had turned an old law
topsy-turvy and made the reversal equally true: greater love
hath no man than this, that he lay down a friend's life for
himself.

Horrible, horrible!

Moira came in, saying, "I left all my money behind, so
I couldn't——" She halted, went wide-eyed, let go a gasp.
"Why, Mr. Harper, what on earth has happened?"

"I had a fit of sneezing."

Dragging his desk upright and restoring his chair to its
legs, he sat and continued to ruminate while Moira scrabbled
for loose papers. Then suddenly he smacked a hand to his
forehead and ejaculated, "I go dafter as I get older!"

He dashed out while Moira knelt in the middle of the
floor and gaped after him.

On the sidewalk Norris and Rausch were standing with
hands in pockets while watching two cruisers speed along
the street.

Norris greeted him with, "He's gone. They'll hand him
over to Leeming in no time." Then a mite doubtfully, "And
I hope you know what you're doing. There'll be plenty of
trouble if we've blundered in this case."

"You've not dealt with the half of it yet," informed Harper
hurriedly. "There's a gang of them hiding in his home.
What's more, I've reason to think they knew of his capture
the moment he was slapped to sleep. Ten to one it got them
on the run forthwith. You'll have to move fast to nab them."

"We can do no more than our best," said Norris unim-
pressed and making no move.

"McDonald's there and several others," Harper urged.

196

He scowled impatiently at the other. "Well, are you going to take action or do I have to go myself?"

"Easy now," Norris advised. He gave a slow smile. "We know exactly where Riley lives. He's been followed time and again."

"What of it?"

"When we carted him out a raid on his house became the next logical step. Five cars with twenty men have gone there. They'll grab everyone they can lay hands on. Afterwards, and if necessary, we'll use you to tell us who is which."

"So you've been thinking ahead of me, eh?"

"It happens sometimes," assured Norris, smiling again. "You can't lead the field all the way. Nobody can do that, no matter what his mental speed."

"Thanks for the reminder. Send a man round the garbage cans to get a few ashes, will you? I wish to put them upon my head while work proceeds."

He returned to the office. Moira had already succeeded in restoring some semblance of order. She filed the last of the scattered papers in the cabinet, closed it with an emphatic slam, surveyed him much as a long-suffering mother would regard an irresponsible child. That did nothing for his ego, either.

"Thank you, Angel. Now go get your lunch."

He waited until she had departed, picked up the phone, made a long-distance call to Leeming.

"A live one is on the way to you right now and, with luck, there'll be several more to come. Don't tell me what you propose to do to the first arrival. I don't want to know."

"Why not?" Leeming asked, exhibiting curiosity through the visiscreen. "Is it somebody close to you?"

"Yes. A big, lumbering, good-natured cop I've known for years. I hate to think of you carving him up."

"He won't be carved. We've done all we need of that on

197

dead bodies. Living victims will be used as test-subjects for likely vaccines."

"What's the chance of developing a satisfactory cure?" Harper asked.

"There's another problem far more important," Leeming gave back. "Namely, whether we can find one in adequate time. We can succeed and yet fail because success comes too late."

"That doesn't answer my question."

"I refuse to commit myself at this stage. We aren't the only ones on the job. In a crisis of this sort, the government turns to anyone and everyone who can lend a hand, private laboratories included. Somebody else may strike lucky and come up with a solution while we're still seeking it. All we can do here is work like hell and pray."

"If producible, an effective vaccine should be innocuous, shouldn't it?" Harper pursued.

"What do you mean?"

"The cure shouldn't be little better than the disease?"

"What the devil are you getting at?"

Harper hesitated, continued carefully, "I'll tell you something. That virus cannot think by itself any more than you can drive a non-existent car. But it can think when in possession of a brain. And I know one thing it thinks about. It is scared to death of meningococci."

"What?" yelled Leeming, thunderstruck.

"I'm giving you a genuine, basic fact. That alien nightmare has a nightmare of its own. No living thing can be afflicted by it and have cerebro-spinal meningitis at one and the same time. Something has to go under and it's the virus that does the going."

"Where did you learn all this?"

"From a victim. The one they're taking down to you at this moment."

"How did you find out?"

"He told me without realizing it. He named his alien obsession and I'm giving it you for what it's worth."

Leeming breathed heavily, excitement showing in his eyes.

"It could be, too. It really could be. Areas of local infection are identical. Brain and spinal column. You can see what that means—a fight for living space."

"Suppose you squirt someone full of meningococci," Harper went on, "and he becomes cured with respect to the foreign disease. What'll he be like with respect to the cure itself?"

"That's something we've yet to discover," said Leeming, grim and determined.

"Well, I've no choice but to leave it with you. All I ask is for you to remember that your first test-subject is my friend."

He cut off, racked the phone, sat twisting his fingers and staring at them. After a while he held his face in his hands and murmured, "It had to be Riley and his wife. Poor devils!"

In the late afternoon Norris beckoned him out of Moira's hearing, said, "They got Mrs. Riley, Mrs. Reed and two men named Farley and Moore. We've discovered that the women are sisters. Farley and Moore were friends of the Reeds. Moore was a close business associate of the Baum brothers. You can see the link-up and how trouble has spread from one to another."

"Did they put up a fight?"

"You bet they did. When the boys got there the house was empty and the front door still swinging. The rats had run for it but hadn't time to escape from sight. Mrs. Riley, Farley and Moore were nabbed on the street half a mile away. They needed three men apiece to hold them."

"And what of the others?" Harper asked.

"Mrs. Reed was picked up in a store pretending to be one of the crowd. She reacted like a wildcat. Reed himself stepped off a roof rather than be taken. McDonald was trapped in a parking lot while trying to steal a car. He was armed. He shot it out to the finish."

"He is dead?"

"Yes. Same as Langley and for the same reason. It was impossible to take him alive."

"How about Gould?"

Norris rocked back. "What d'you mean, how about Gould?"

"He was there at Riley's house."

"Are you sure of that?"

"I'm positive."

Accepting that without argument, Norris affirmed, "There was no sign of him. But he'll be found." He mused a bit, went on, "We're now tracing all contacts of the entire bunch and pulling them in as fast as we find them. The total number may come to hundreds. Anyone known to have stood within a yard of any one of them is liable to be taken for questioning. You'd better hold yourself in readiness to look them over as we line them up."

"All right."

"It may go on for weeks, perhaps months."

"I'll suffer it." Harper eyed him speculatively. "You say that Riley's house was deserted when your men arrived?"

"Yes."

"Who tipped them to leave in a hurry?"

"Nobody," said Norris. "When Riley didn't return on time they took alarm and fled."

"It was more positive than that," Harper informed. "They were tipped."

"By whom?"

"By Riley himself. He couldn't help it. He lost consciousness and that was enough for them. They got out fast the moment one of your boys clouted Riley on the head. They *knew* he'd been caught."

"I don't see how," Norris protested.

"Never mind how. I'm telling you that each one of them knows when another has been put out of action."

"What of it, anyway?"

"At the Bio. Lab. they're holding an afflicted dog. I've a feeling that sooner or later that animal may be able to summon help. It's a guess and nothing more. How about persuading Jameson to put a guard on the place?"

"It's already protected. You ought to know that. You've been there."

"The guard is a military one. It isn't prepared for the sort of trouble we're having here."

"You're doing the identification for us at this end," said Norris. "Who'll do it for them down there?"

"Me."

"What, over such a distance?"

"I'm going there. I'm a constant centre of interest to the foe no matter where I may be. That dog is a focal point for them. So is each and every live victim we hold. Get them all in one place and we thereby create a cumulative attraction that may prove irresistible. Desire for revenge, rescue and continued concealment should be more than enough to draw the enemy's full strength to the one spot. Their best bet lies in making a concerted effort. It would be about the only chance we'd ever get of settling them with a single blow."

"I'll put it to Jameson and ask him to consult General Conway," said Norris. "The plan is worth considering."

"While you're at it you can tell Jameson that I'm on my way, no matter what is decided."

"You can't do that."

"I can. Try giving me contrary orders and see where it gets you." He grinned at Norris. "I'm a free individual and intend to remain one with or without the kind permission of Conway or any other character."

"But Rausch and I have to stay with you," Norris objected. "And we're supposed to work this trap. It's operating all right. Look at today's catch."

"The bait is transferring itself to a bigger and better rat-run," Harper gave back. "Please yourself whether you come along."

He tramped into the office, found his week-end case, checked its contents, said to Moira, "Hold the fort, rush out the products, make excuses for me and bank the profits. Papa's taking another trip."

Norris and Rausch piled into his car as he was about to start, and the former said, "We've got to hang on to your coat-tails, no matter what you do. Your plant remains under guard. But if someone cockeyed walks into it there'll be nobody to give warning."

"Same applies at the Bio. Lab., which is now a more enticing target." Harper pulled out from the kerb and took the centre of the street. "And I cannot be in two places at once."

He drove fast with another burdened car following close behind. His mind reached out and felt around as he went through the town. This time, he decided, a faint threnody of alien thoughts would not be ignored. He was at the wheel and he'd go after it.

But it did not come. They cleared the town and roared into the country without being drawn into hectic pursuit of a lone masquerader among the multitude. That did not mean that Gould or any fellow conspirators had fled the place; only that if still there they were lurking out of receptive range.

The car swung into its fenced and patrolled destination an hour after darkness had fallen. Norris immediately put through a call to Jameson, briefed him on latest events. Some time later Jameson called back.

"You're getting your own way," Norris informed Harper. "Conway has ordered special measures to protect this place."

"Unless I've gravely miscalculated, we'll need 'em."

They did.

The attack came four days afterwards, by which time the

delay had given some the secret belief that nothing would ever happen. It employed a technique characteristic of alien-controlled minds filled with two-world data and trying to combine the tactics of both. The plan represented a compromise between sneakiness and direct assault.

At midday a large, official-looking car slid up to the gates barring the main entrance. Its driver was attired as a sergeant of military police and its sole passenger was a grey-haired, autocratic man in the uniform of a four-star general. The sergeant showed the sentry an imposing pass, stamped, signed and ornamented with a large seal. The sentry scanned it slowly, making no attempt to open the gates. He smelled eucalyptus.

"Hurry up, Mister!" urged the sergeant authoritatively, while the general gazed forth with an air of stern reproof.

Though made nervous by the presence of high rank, the sentry took his time. He had been well-trained these last few days and understood that the gates were barred to God himself unless a bell in a nearby hut clanged permission to enter.

The bell did not sound. In the hut, at back of the fence, a watching agent pressed a stud. And in a building a quarter of a mile away a buzzer drew Harper's attention to the gate. He heard the whirr, ceased conversation with Rausch, listened, pressed another stud. A shrill peep sounded from the hut and an alarm siren started wailing over the main building.

Startled, the sentry dropped the pass, levelled his gun at the sergeant. Four agents leaped from the hut, weapons in hands. A dozen more appeared in the roadway behind the car.

Once more the possessed displayed their inhuman contempt for bullets and sudden death. Without slightest change of expression the sergeant let the car charge forward. The sentry fired two seconds before the bonnet struck his chest. The car hit the gate squarely in the middle and exploded.

The gate, the entire front of the hut, the car, its occupants, the sentry and six agents flew to pieces. Four more agents lay mauled and dead. Six groaned by the fence, injured but alive.

Two heavily loaded cars screamed along the road and rocked through the gap. The wounded agents fired into them as they passed, without visible result.

Neither vehicle got more than twenty yards beyond the wrecked gateway despite the lunatic speed with which they had arived. The alarm had sounded too promptly, the preparations for it were too good, the drill too well-organized.

The leading car found its route blocked by an eighty-ton tank which lumbered forward spewing fire from three loopholes, riddling the target at the rate of two thousand bullets per minute. Shedding glass, metal splinters and blood, it slewed on to grass and overturned. Nothing stirred within it.

Its follower halted just inside the fence, disgorged eight men who spread fanwise and raced inward at an angle outside the arc of fire. Ignoring them, the tank busily wrecked their machine.

Something farther back gave a low, dull *whoompwhoomp* and spurts of heavy vapour sprang from the ground one jump ahead of the invading eight. It did not halt them or give them to pause. They pelted headlong through the curtain of mist, made another twenty yards, collapsed one by one.

A pair of them dropped clutching grenades in hands that lost grip as vapour compelled their minds to swirl into unconsciousness. Released plungers walloped detonators, there came two brief eruptions of turf, dirt and flesh.

Masked men picked up the remaining six as the tank crunched forward on noisy caterpillars and filled the torn gateway. Shots and shouts sounded far away at the other side of the area where six men had picked off two patrolling guards, climbed the fence and been trapped. It was a foolhardy tactic depending for success in sufficient diversion at the front gate.

Five minutes after the battle had ended a convoy of armoured cars toured the countryside for fifty miles around, Harper being a passenger in the first one. It was two hours before he picked up the only trace.

"There!" he said, pointing to an abandoned farmhouse.

They kept him out of reach while they made the attack. It produced three corpses and two badly wounded captives.

No more were findable before dawn, when the search became complete. Harper arrived back red-eyed, tousle-haired and fed up.

"Gould was in that first car," Norris informed.

"Dead?"

"All of them, nine in number. That tank made a job of it." He shrugged, added, "Now we've the task of discovering the identities of all those involved, including those whose bodies got scattered around. After that, we must trace all their contacts and bring them in for clearance by you. I can see this lasting my lifetime."

Leeming entered the room. He was pale and drawn from lack of sleep. He said to Harper, "I'd like you to come take a look."

Leading the other through a series of corridors in which an armed guard stood at every corner, he reached a row of strongly barred cells, pointed into one.

"What can you tell me?" he asked in strained and anxious tones.

Harper looked. Inside, clad only in socks and pants, Riley sat aimlessly on the edge of a bed. His eyes were lacklustre but his beefy face held an expression of childish amusement.

"Well?" pressed Leeming. "Is the virus conquered?"

"Yes." He voiced it without triumph and the other heard it without joy.

"You can say positively that it is no longer active within his system?"

"Yes."

Leeming hesitated, spoke solemnly. "I gave him what you said he feared the most. We had to try it. We just can't wait for a vaccine. First things come first—and humanity comes before the individual. So I called in Gottlieb and Mathers of the Bacteriological Warfare Station and we tried it."

Harper made no remark.

"It has proved a cure," Leeming went on. "Physically there are no ill effects. He shows no symptoms of meningitis from that viewpoint. Nevertheless, he has paid a price. I know it but I want your confirmation." He looked at Harper as if hoping for the one chance in a thousand that he would be pronounced wrong. "What is the price?"

"Insanity," said Harper.

"I hate to hear you say it." Leeming stood silently awhile and tasted the bitter ashes of victory, then said with faint hope, "There's another one in the next cell. A fellow named Moore."

Harper went there, gazed in and declared, "The same." Then something inside him gave way and he growled, "They're better off dead. Do you hear me? They have minds like porridge, all messed up to hell, and they're better off dead."

"They are dead," informed Leeming, on the defence. "They were dead when first brought to me. I cannot restore a human spirit already lost, I cannot recall an expelled soul. Science has its limits. When it can get that far it will have ceased to be science. The best we can manage is to defend the community by destroying a source of infection. And that we have achieved."

"I know, I know. Don't think I'm blaming you or anyone else." He patted Leeming's shoulder by way of comfort. "And don't reproach yourself, either. It's my illogical habit to regret the dirtier facts of life even when they're unalterable."

"Everything that can be done will be done," assured Leeming, perking up slightly. "We're treating all of them in the same way because at least it's swift and sure. After that, some of the country's best mental specialists will take them over. That's right out of my field but I wouldn't say they're beyond help. Maybe others can restore them to normality."

"Never," asserted Harper. "A battlefield is a torn and sterile area pock-marked with craters, littered with rubble and stinking of decomposition. That's what their brains are like."

He walked away, twitching fingers as he went. The war for a world had been won because, as usual, the few had sacrificed themselves for the many. The few who were humanity's best. Always it had been so, always would be.

It was two years before the last echoes of combat died away. That was when they called upon him to inspect and pass judgment on a small group of frightened people finally run down in faraway places. These were the only remaining contacts with any of the possessed. None proved subject to otherworld mastery.

During that long time he had looked over more than eight thousand suspects, many of them shipped back from overseas by co-operation of warned and wary governments. In the first week he had discovered four men who were not men, and in the second week one woman who was not a woman. After that there had been no more. The world had cleared itself of mental sepsis.

The missing space-vessel had been discovered lying in a hundred fathoms beyond Puget Sound, and salvage outfits were still toiling to raise it piecemeal. Scientists were busily devising positive means of protection for a second Venusian expedition and seeking an effective weapon with which to free the Wends, an agile, intelligent, lemur-like creature that could speak.

"Var silvin, Wend?"

The Lunar Development Company had won its suit and the powers-that-be had received a legalistic rap across the knuckles. A reward of five thousand dollars had been used to start a fund for the dependents of spacemen and already the total sum had passed the million mark. From Harper's viewpoint, these were by far the two most pleasing items to date.

But no heavy hand bashed open his door, nobody brushed his papers aside to make seating room on his desk, nobody claimed some of his time for an exchange of insults. Riley was away in a big house in the country, helping with the gardening, doing petty chores, smiling at chirping sparrows, being gently led to his bedroom when sleepy time came. Like all the others, a little child. He would never be any different. Never, never, never.

So far as Harper personally was concerned, the after-effects of the fracas would remain with him all his life. Not only in memory but also in immediate circumstances.

For instance, business had grown as he expanded into ancillary products. Forty men now worked in the plant. One of them, Weiss, was not only a highly skilled instrument maker, but also a government stooge. Conway's eye. He could blind it by firing the man—only to be watched by another. There was no way of getting rid of constant observation.

His mail was watched. There were many times when he suspected a tap on his telephone line. Whenever he made a swift move by car or plane he was followed. Norris or Rausch called once a month for an idle chat designed to remind him that the memory of authority is long and unforgiving.

What they were after was continued proof of his genuine uniqueness to the end of his days or, alternatively, evidence that birds of a feather were beginning to flock together. One

Harper was enough. Two would be dangerous. Ten would represent a major crisis.

Despite rapidly increasing prosperity he was irritable, frustrated and desperately lonely. He experienced all the soul-searing solitude of a rare animal in the zoo constantly stared at by numberless curious eyes. Sometimes he felt that they'd willingly shoot him and stuff him but for the remote possibility of a recurrence of past events. They might need him again.

Yes, they feared him, but feared other things more.

There was no escape from the situation other than that of burying himself in business, of concentrating on one thing to the exclusion of everything else. That he had done to the best of his ability. So the plant had grown and micromanipulators become only a minor part of his output. He was heading for the role of a wealthy man locked in a worldwide jail.

Another thirty months crawled by, making four and a half years in all. Then the miracle happened. It was unbelievable. But it was true.

He was about to take his car from a parking lot when he caught a brief flicker of alien thought. It struck him like a physical blow. The direction and range were sensed automatically: from the south, about four miles away. A distance far beyond his normal receptivity.

With sweating hand on the car's door he stood and listened again, seeking it directively. There it came. It was not alien. It had only seemed to be so because new and strange, like nothing previously encountered. It had power and clarity as different from other thought-streams as champagne differs from water.

He probed at it and immediately it came back with shock equal to his own. Getting into his car, he sat there shakily. His mind fizzed with excitement and there were butterflies in his stomach while he remained staring through the wind-

209

shield and apparently day-dreaming. Finally, he drove to a large restaurant, ordered dinner.

She had a table to herself far away at the opposite end of the room. A strawberry blonde, small, plump, in her middle thirties. Her face was pleasantly freckled and she had a tip-tilted nose. At no time did she glance his way. Neither did he pay any attention to her when he departed.

After that they met frequently without ever coming near each other or exchanging one vocal word. Sometimes he ate in one place while she sipped coffee in another half a mile away. Other times he mused absently in the office while she became thoughtful in a distant store. They took in the same show, he in one part of the theatre and she in another, and neither saw much of the performance.

They were waiting, waiting for circumstances to change with enough naturalness and inevitability to fool the watchers. The opportunity was coming, they both knew that. Moira was wearing a diamond ring.

In due course Moira departed with congratulations and a wedding gift. Twenty girls answered the call for her successor. Harper interviewed them all, according the same courtesy, putting the same questions, displaying no visible favouritism one way or the other.

He chose Frances, a strawberry blonde with plump figure and pert nose.

Ten days later Norris arrived on his periodic visit, looked over the newcomer, favoured her with a pleasant smile, mentally defined her as nice and nothing more. He started the chit-chat while Harper listened and gazed dreamily at a point behind the other's back.

"For the fiftieth time, will you marry me?"

"For the fiftieth time, yes. But you must be patient. We'll fall into it gradually."

"So this fellow showed the manager a bunch of documents certifying him to be a bank manager from head office," droned Norris. "The manager fell for it and——" He paused, added in louder tones, "Hey! Are you paying attention?"

"Of course. Carry on. I can hardly wait for the climax."

"I don't want to be patient. I don't want to be gradual. I want to fall into it fast."

"You know better than that. We must be careful."

"I want children just like us."

"Wait!"

She slipped paper into her typewriter, adjusted it, pink-faced and smiling.

"That was his downfall," finished Norris, completely innocent of the by-play. "So he tied himself up for life."

"Don't we all?" said Harper, hiding his bliss.

THE END

There's an epidemic with 27 million victims. And no visible symptoms.

It's an epidemic of people who can't read.

Believe it or not, 27 million Americans are functionally illiterate, about one adult in five.

The solution to this problem is you... when you join the fight against illiteracy. So call the Coalition for Literacy at toll-free **1-800-228-8813** and volunteer.

**Volunteer
Against Illiteracy.
The only degree you need
is a degree of caring.**

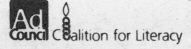

Ad Council Coalition for Literacy

LV-1